A Candlelight Ecstasy Romance ®

DEFTLY, WITH A SKILL THAT SURPRISED HER, HE UNDID HER HAIR AND COMBED THE STRANDS FREE WITH HIS FINGERS.

"Like silk," he murmured when her ebony hair lay loosely about her shoulders. "Dark, midnight silk."

"Y-you don't sound like a football player. . . ." Karla whispered, hardly aware of what she was saying.

"Forget that part of me," he rasped. "I'm a man, that's all."

That was enough, Karla thought dimly as his head moved slowly down toward her. Oh, Lord! It was more than enough. She was drowning in feeling. Not even the soaring ecstasy of the prima ballerina's solo in *Swan Lake* or the aching beauty of the pas de deux in *Romeo and Juliet* had prepared her. . . .

A CANDLELIGHT ECSTASY ROMANCE ®

GAME PLAN

Sara Jennings

A CANDLELIGHT ECSTASY ROMANCE ®

Published by
Dell Publishing Co., Inc.
1 Dag Hammarskjold Plaza
New York, New York 10017

Dell ® TM 681510, Dell Publishing Co., Inc.

Candlelight Ecstasy Romance®, 1,203,540, is a registered
trademark of Dell Publishing Co., Inc., New York,
New York.

ISBN: 0-440-12791-2

Printed in the United States of America

First printing—July 1984

To Our Readers:

We have been delighted with your enthusiastic response to Candlelight Ecstasy Romances®, and we thank you for the interest you have shown in this exciting series.

In the upcoming months we will continue to present the distinctive sensuous love stories you have come to expect only from Ecstasy. We look forward to bringing you many more books from your favorite authors and also the very finest work from new authors of contemporary romantic fiction.

As always, we are striving to present the unique, absorbing love stories that you enjoy most—books that are more than ordinary romance.

Your suggestions and comments are always welcome. Please write to us at the address below.

Sincerely,

The Editors
Candlelight Romances
1 Dag Hammarskjold Plaza
New York, New York 10017

CHAPTER ONE

"No way I'm going in there, man! The whole thing's stupid! I'm not some *pansy*!"

The deep, angry voice outside the exercise room door made Karla Morley stiffen. She hadn't expected her first day as ballet trainer to the New York Flyers football team to be easy, but neither had she anticipated the animosity she felt pouring out at her from the other side of the door.

Sighing, she took a deep breath and straightened her shoulders. The first few minutes were going to be the roughest. She might as well just get them over with quickly.

Taking a swift glance at herself in the wall of mirrors, she confirmed that her appearance was properly professional. Her midnight black hair was swept up in a neat knot at the back of her long, slender neck. The light blue leotard and tights she wore matched her large, thick-fringed eyes. Her classic features were deceptively delicate. Only the stubborn set of her chin hinted at her determination. It contrasted provocatively with the sensual curve of her full mouth.

At twenty-six, she was a seasoned veteran of the ballet. Lead dancer at City Center, respected choreographer, internationally renowned soloist. She didn't need this job with the Flyers—she'd accepted it only as a favor to the team's owner, who was an old friend, and because of the challenge it presented.

Nodding at herself in the mirror, she silently confirmed her resolve not to put up with any nonsense. There might be big, tough football players on the other side of that door, but they were *losing* players and it was her job to change that.

"Management's gone out of its skull," another voice declared. "Treating us like a bunch of limp-wrists. What the hell are they trying to do to us!"

"Cool down, Dave," someone said, more quietly than the others. "This isn't as crazy as it sounds. This—what's her name?—Morley is just going to improve our coordination." There was a low, mocking laugh. "You've got to admit, we could use some help."

"Not this kind! How are we supposed to hold our heads up once this gets out? Hell, I can hear it now. Instead of the Flyers, everyone'll be calling us the Fairies!"

"So what? What do you care what anyone says about us? We're still the best damn team in football, and it's time we remembered that. If this broad can help us, more power to her."

Broad? Karla scowled. Just when she had begun to think the owner of the deep voice might be an ally, he blew it. She had no patience, and even less respect,

10

for men who thought of women in such terms. Yanking open the door, she said coldly, "If you're quite through expressing your opinions, *gentlemen,* we have work to do."

Two dozen pairs of eyes locked on her. Karla caught a glimpse of their varying reactions—surprise, resentment, defiance—before her own impressions swamped her.

She felt as though she had wandered into an immense forest, except that the trees were human. At five feet six inches, she had never thought of herself as small. But compared to these titans, she was tiny. She actually had to crane her neck back to see the top of them.

To make matters more overwhelming, each man was as well built as he was tall. Massive shoulders, broad chests, sinewy hips, and ripcord-taut thighs filled her vision.

The football game she had watched on television the previous weekend in preparation for her new job had not readied her in any way for this confrontation. On the screen, the players had looked if not small, then of at least manageable proportions. Up close, she was forced to admit nothing could be further from the truth.

With the exception of the two coaches, all the men were dressed in gray sweat shirts and pants emblazoned with the Flyers logo. Karla dimly remembered something about there being eleven of them on the offense team and the same number on defense. At least they all seemed to have turned up. Lucky her.

Her cheeks darkened, and a dangerous gleam entered her eyes as she realized they were subjecting her to the same scrutiny she had given them. Being a professional dancer, she was used to being looked at. But the genteel regard of an audience was quite different from what she was receiving from these men.

"Whoo-ee," a sandy-haired behemoth exclaimed. "Would you get a load of this little gal. Looks like a puff of wind could blow her away." Squatting down until he could look her in the eye, he grinned at her tauntingly. "Honey, why don't you just turn around and take that cute little butt of yours out of here before you get eat up by a big bad wolf!"

The other men chuckled appreciatively, egging him on. Karla groaned inwardly but refused to give an inch. Frost clung to her voice as she glanced at the name stitched on his sweat shirt, then she said slowly and distinctly, "There are two ways we can do this, Johanssen, the tough way and the easy way. I've got six weeks to teach you something about coordination. Believe me, I can make it seem like six years."

Turning, she pointed toward the exercise room. "And I will"—her voice tightened ominously—"unless you forget about my butt and get yours in there *pronto!*"

Dead silence. The coaches looked at each other in horror. The face of her challenger turned bright red. He drew in his breath sharply and moved his feet back and forth in place, almost like a huge animal pawing the ground. "Lady," he grated harshly, "you're looking for a—"

"Take it easy, Mike." Stepping between the pair, the owner of the deep voice placed his hand on the other player's arm and spoke to him quietly.

Karla's eyes widened as she realized her defender was Mac Gregor, quarterback of the Flyers, darling

12

of the media, and—if reputation was anything to go on—collector of beautiful women who were only too happy to share both his glamorous life-style and his bed.

His photos didn't do him justice. Where many of the other men were so big as to be lumbering, he was lithe and sinewy. Her dancer's eye couldn't help but notice the fluid beauty of his body even as the woman in her responded to the broad sweep of powerful muscles and the aura of steely strength unmistakable even in his present garb.

Craggy features and a nose that looked as though it had been broken at least once only added to his virile charm. Chestnut hair tumbled across his broad forehead in a beguiling artlessness she tried to tell herself was the work of a high-priced stylist.

Her attempt at cynicism failed miserably. Mesmerized by the impact of sherry-hued eyes, she came down to earth abruptly when he said, "Don't let a little thing like her get your dander up. Hell, she's no more than a 'skeeter buzzing around a bull!"

Karla waited until the laughter died away and her anger was sufficiently under control before she said sweetly, "A few minutes ago, Mr. Gregor, I was a 'broad.' Just for the record, the name is Morley, and I'll thank you to remember it."

She paused for a moment, taking in his surprised look, before adding, "Much as I'd love to stand around and chat, we do have work to do. So if you all wouldn't mind . . ." With exaggerated politeness, she once again pointed the way into the exercise room.

Prodded by the coaches who were on hand for just that purpose, the men sullenly tromped inside. Only

Mac hung back, studying her with a speculative gleam that made her stomach tighten. Determined to ignore him, she started to walk past.

A hand shot out, so quickly that she never even saw it coming. Gripped gently but firmly, she was stopped in midstride.

"What the . . . let go of me!"

"In a second," he said calmly. "First I want to give you a piece of advice." When she continued to glare at him, he added, "It's obvious you know who I am, so you should have enough sense to listen to me. As quarterback of this team, I know every man on it as well as I know my own brothers. And believe me, lady, unless you come down off that high horse of yours, you're going to be in trouble."

Karla opened her mouth to deliver a sharp retort, only to lose track of what she had meant to say. The touch of his warm, strong fingers on her skin sent startling shivers of pleasure radiating through her.

Bewildered, she stared down at the burnished hand holding her, then back to the piercing eyes studying her flushed face.

Her mouth tightened grimly. Accustomed to being in complete control of her body, she found her response to him both disquieting and distasteful. Never had a man's touch affected her so intensely.

Admittedly, her experience was limited. In the grueling world of the ballet, there was little time or opportunity to develop relationships. On occasion, she had regretted that. Now she saw it had advantages. The last thing she needed in her life was to tangle with an overly libidinous jock!

Tight-lipped, she looked him straight in the eye as she said quietly, "You and your teammates are welcome to try to get rid of me, but I'll tell you right now you won't succeed. You'd be smarter to save your energy for the workouts, where you're going to need it. Now let go of my arm. You're hurting me."

In her annoyance at the events of the last few minutes, she had failed to notice that she and Mac were the focal point of attention. Every member of the team was watching them with avid interest, waiting to see how their quarterback would handle the situation.

Whatever they'd expected, they ended up disappointed. With a muffled curse, he dropped his hand and turned his back on her, striding over to join the other men.

There was a long, tense moment of silence before Karla said wryly, "Since I seem to have your attention, I'll take this opportunity to explain what we'll be doing here and why it can help your game."

Standing by herself in the front of the room, she briefly described how dance combined strength and agility with precise timing. "I know you think what I do is easy"—she smiled slightly—"so much so that you can't imagine a real man involved in it. But believe me, ballet is a lot tougher than you think." She paused for a moment and smiled again, this time with a hint of anticipation. "As you are about to discover."

Certain now that she had at least managed to capture their interest, she asked the men to line up next to the bar. They hesitated, but a warning glare from the coaches and a muttered reminder that fines would be levied against anyone who failed to cooperate convinced them to go along, grudgingly.

After running down the list of names and double-checking with the coaches to make sure she understood which men were recovering from injuries, she began to put them through a few simple exercises to loosen muscles and stretch tendons.

It came as no surprise to discover, even at this very early stage, that the men had a variety of techniques for expressing their resentment and anger. Most affected great boredom, making it clear they felt the simple exercises were child's play.

A few deliberately worked out of sync, making each movement just a split second slower than it should have been. Several began to talk loudly among themselves, beginning a highly graphic discussion of several women they knew.

When none of these tactics had the slightest effect on Karla, one of the pass receivers was driven to address her directly. Jeeringly he said, "I hope they're not paying you much for this, lady. It sure ain't worth it!"

The other men laughed, but Karla merely smiled. "I get paid for results, Wolanski. Too bad the same can't be said for you."

His mouth dropped open as he stopped stock-still. "Why, you . . ."

Karla faced him calmly. She had decided the moment he started in on her that she had no choice but to go on the offensive. The players' opposition to her had to be stopped before it got completely out of hand.

"Can't you take it?" she asked with deceptive softness. "You seem willing enough to dish it out. How does it feel to have signed a six-figure contract last year and hardly caught the ball since? Your teammates must be getting tired of throwing to empty air."

"Lady, I'm warning you . . ."

Hands on her hips, Karla stood her ground as the player strode up to her, stopping only when his huge chest was practically pushing against her nose. Though her stomach tightened and her heart beat painfully, she refused to show the least sign of fear.

Meeting him glare for glare, she said, "Save it, Wolanski. You've got enough problems without trying to take me on. Now get back in line and stretch!"

For a long, tense moment, they stared at each other, neither willing to give an inch. At last, the player muttered a foul imprecation and stomped back to the bar.

There was a collective sigh of relief, during which Karla could not help but notice Mac staring at her grimly. His fists were clenched at his sides, and he looked poised to leap into trouble. With a start, she realized he had expected to have to save her from the irate Wolanski.

Surprisingly touched by his concern, Karla moved to lighten the situation. Grinning unabashedly she said, "I guess I should have warned you that my dad was a marine. He taught me that in a showdown the worst thing you can do is blink."

Even Wolanski laughed at that, if a bit grudgingly. "He must have taught you good," a linebacker muttered. "You sure don't scare easy."

In the slightly less tense mood that followed that acknowledgment, the men were a little more cooperative. Not much, but enough for her to believe there might be hope for the project after all.

As she moved down the line of men, offering encouragement and quiet correction, she was acutely aware of Mac watching her. It took all her discipline not to return his scrutiny. The brief glimpses she allowed herself confirmed that he was in magnificent condition.

At six and a half feet tall, he easily carried some two hundred pounds, not an ounce of it fat. His agility and stamina were impressive even to a dancer.

But once again, he mostly affected the woman in her. She could not shake the memory of his touch, nor the vague, undefined longings it had set off in her. At one point, she caught herself wondering what it would be like to be held in his arms, cradled against his massive chest.

Annoyed, she dragged her errant thoughts back to the business at hand and concentrated firmly on the exercises.

By the time she finally called a halt forty-five minutes later, the gray sweat suits were streaked with perspiration, and there were bewildered looks in the eyes watching her.

She swallowed a grin as she realized how surprised they were by the vigor of a dance workout. It was safe to say the starch had definitely been taken out of twenty-two backbones.

No, make that twenty-one. Mac looked as though he'd done nothing more than run a few laps. In fact, he seemed ready, willing, and able to go all day.

Shooting her a mocking grin, he drawled, "Is that it? I was just starting to get warmed up."

"Good," she told him tartly. "Then you'll be all set for tomorrow when we really get going."

The men groaned as she briskly read off the schedule for workouts. "An hour every day, gentlemen. Same time, same place." Picking up her towel, she slipped it around her neck and headed for the private locker room designated for her use. At the door, she turned back for a moment and smiled sympathetically. "If it's any consolation, I'm going straight from here to ballet class and a *real* work-out."

"You gotta be made of steel, lady," one of the men murmured. Karla heard him and laughed, but didn't turn back again. She thought she had accomplished a great deal from that difficult beginning but didn't want to push her luck too far.

Mac watched her go thoughtfully, his eyes on the long line of her legs and the curve of her bottom. A wry grin lit his eyes. Her slender, willowy body was markedly different from the voluptuousness he usually favored, yet its impact was greater than he could ever have anticipated. Maybe his tastes were changing.

An interesting thought, but just then he had more pressing concerns. The moment she was gone he sagged against the wall, his macho pose evaporating. "Sweet lord, I hurt in places I didn't know I had!"

"You said you were just getting warmed up," a blocker kidded.

"Who were you trying to impress, Mac? The little lady?"

"The little lady," he muttered, "makes a drill sergeant look like a girl scout." He shook his head dazedly. How anything so soft and pretty could be so hard-nosed was beyond him.

The first sight of her had hit him like a ton of bricks. He'd been completely unprepared for the dazzling combination of beauty, intelligence, and grace she represented. His first instinct had been to protect her, and he hadn't hesitated to act on it.

The big shock had come when he discovered she didn't need his help. Considering that there were grown men who would run in the opposite direction from an irate football player, her behavior was astonishing. Not only was she the sexiest thing he'd come across in a long time, but she had more than her share of guts.

Which left him . . . where? Honesty rather than pride made him acknowledge that he generally had his way with any member of the fair sex his eye happened to fall upon. His looks and personality were enough by themselves to assure his success, but when combined with his wealth and fame, they made him all but irresistible.

In the last several years, he had enjoyed a series of liaisons with lovely ladies, all of whom knew the score as well as he did. He'd had a hell of a lot of good times, steering clear of any woman who even hinted at something more serious than a brief fling.

But he'd always been scrupulously honest about his intentions. More than once, he'd walked away from a situation he knew would lead to pain for the other party. He made no apologies for his life-style, but neither did he ever knowingly hurt anyone.

So how come he'd felt lately that it just wasn't worth the effort to go on this way? He was living the dream of a good portion of the male population. Why wasn't he enjoying it more?

Stepping under the shower in the players' locker room, he shook his head impatiently. He'd never gone in for self-analysis and couldn't understand why he was indulging in it now.

A humorless smile curved his firm mouth. His oldest brother, Tad, thought he knew the reason. "Face it," Tad had advised the last time they had dinner together, "you're finally growing up. It happens to the best of us."

Mac still hadn't figured out what that meant, but he suspected it had something to do with the woman Tad had been dating for several months. All the Gregor brothers had a fondness for variety, Tad included. It had come as quite a shock, therefore, to realize Tad had stopped seeing anyone but Jeannie.

Tad would be getting married soon, Mac suspected. At thirty-five, he had given in to the desire for a real home and family. It wouldn't be surprising if he was a father before too long.

His smile softened. That would make him an uncle. Not too hard to take. He liked kids. He spent a good portion of his free time with them. He wouldn't mind being a father himself someday. If he found the right woman, of course.

Karla's face swam before him. The cold water pounding across his big, taut body seemed suddenly warm. She was something, all right. What exactly, he wasn't sure. But he had a feeling he was going to find out.

On the other side of the wall, the object of his thoughts listened to the rush of water as she toweled her hair dry. With the discipline that was an inbred part of her life, she tried to keep her mind firmly on business.

It had gone better than she had expected. The men were surly and upset, but they weren't completely unreasonable. They respected determination and courage, and she had plenty of both.

A soft laugh escaped her as she stood in front of the mirror and turned the hair dryer on. Looking at the situation from their point of view, she had to admit she must have come as quite a shock to them. They seemed to have only one use for women and it wasn't teaching ballet!

Unbidden, the thought of Mac Gregor rose to cloud her thoughts. Was he as much like the others as he seemed, or had the brief glimpse of concern she had seen in his eyes been genuine?

Not that it mattered. There couldn't be anything between them except a strictly businesslike relationship. She was a dedicated dancer, at the peak of her career. She lived for her art and had since the age of six when she took her first lessons.

Her entire existence was wrapped up in the ballet. She came alive fully only on stage, during those incandescent moments when she soared with the music.

Surely nothing a mere man could offer could possibly equal what she experienced when she danced? Or could it . . . ?

Lately, she had felt the first faint stirrings of dissatisfaction, questions about her life's purpose, uncertainty about where she was going. The doubts were still muted and indistinct but nonetheless startling in the face of her previous single-minded determination.

She must just be tired. Her schedule was grueling, and taking on the Flyers class had only worsened it. She really should give some thought to a vacation.

Maybe in a few months, in the winter, she could get away to someplace warm.

In the meantime, there was too much to do to be wasting time. Brushing her ebony tresses, she glanced at the wall clock. Half an hour before she was due in class. After class, a quick break for dinner before a choreography meeting. She would be lucky to get to bed by midnight and had to get up at six A.M. to begin the whole thing over again.

A wry smile lit her eyes as she pulled on a wool skirt and a bulky knit sweater. The life of a dancer. It was all she had ever wanted. It still was . . . wasn't it?

Taking a quick look around to make sure she hadn't forgotten anything, she flicked off the light and hurried out. The corridor was empty. Hurrying down it, she was aware of the deep voices coming from the players' locker room.

As she turned the corner toward the exit, she thought she heard Mac's laugh. For just an instant, she hesitated, struck by the sudden desire to see him again.

But she would, tomorrow. And the next day and the next, for six weeks. On a purely professional level, which was exactly what she wanted.

Wasn't it?

CHAPTER TWO

"You look marvelous, sweetheart. I'm glad you could make it."

Karla smiled warmly at the older man who had risen the moment she entered the small, exclusive restaurant. She slipped off the persimmon-colored wool jacket she wore over a matching skirt and taupe turtleneck, tossed her long, ebony braid over her shoulder, and accepted a light kiss on the cheek from her companion before she sat down in the chair held for her by the maitre d'.

Brad Harris was the soul of gallantry. At fifty-six, his robust, silver-haired frame was still vigorous enough to catch any woman's eye. But he remained faithful to the memory of his late wife, concentrating all his enormous energy on his far-flung business empire. An empire that included the Flyers football team.

"So how did it go?" Brad inquired just a bit anxiously as she sat down and gave her order for a drink to the waiter.

"Not as badly as it might have," Karla said reassuringly. "The players are hardly thrilled, but once they realized I wouldn't turn tail and run, they settled down pretty well."

"I'll bet they did." Brad laughed. "What I would have given to be there today!" He paused for a moment before adding more seriously, "If you remember, I offered to go with you."

"I know, but it was best that you didn't. The situation's tough enough without having you on hand to remind the players that they have no choice but to cooperate."

"Still, I was worried about how you'd be treated. The guys can be a little rough sometimes."

"So can I," she reminded him firmly. Ever since her father's death five years before, Brad had shown a tendency to be overly protective toward her. As an honorary uncle who had known her since birth, he undoubtedly felt he had the right. Karla deeply appreciated his concern, but that didn't mean she was going to let him treat her like a child.

Brad threw back his head and laughed, attracting appreciative glances from several nearby women. "You're so much like your dad it's amazing. All anyone had to do was tell Sam something was too much for him, and he'd be sure to wade right into it. Come out smelling like a rose, too. All the years I knew him, I never saw him flop once."

"He was a wonderful father," Karla said softly. "I still miss him."

"I'm sorry, honey." A burnished hand reached out

to touch hers gently. "I didn't mean to bring up sad memories."

"No, that's all right."

"You've got a lot of your mother in you, too," Brad said admiringly. "She was one hell of a lady."

"So you've told me." Karla was silent for a moment, thinking about her mother. She barely remembered her. Natalia Morley had died when her daughter was six, leaving a grief-stricken husband to cope with raising a child alone. He had succeeded admirably but had always said that he couldn't have done it without the help of good friends like Brad.

"I remember a few months after Momma died," she said softly, "when I told Dad I wanted to take ballet lessons. I had no idea how painful it would be for him to see me following in her footsteps. He never let on for a moment. All those years, he stuck by me completely."

"He was immensely proud of you. You were the best of two fine races." He grinned warmly. "Irish and Russian, what a combination. It's inevitable that you should set off fireworks."

"Is that what I do?" Karla asked impishly. Her single glass of wine and the indulgence of a really good steak were making her feel better than she had in weeks. Some of the tension built up over the long, trying day eased from her.

"You know you do. When you're up on the stage, you enthrall an audience."

"You're my biggest fan," she said lightly, embarrassed as always by his praise. "I know I can do a good job in front of an audience, but away from there . . ." Her voice trailed off.

26

Brad frowned slightly. "I'm not sure I understand."

She smiled apologetically. "Forgive me. I'm not making much sense this evening. What I meant is that I've been so caught up in the ballet since childhood that it must be impossible to imagine me involved with anything else."

Brad put his drink down, his eyes suddenly serious as he said, "No, Karla, it isn't impossible at all. I just haven't wanted to broach the subject because I wasn't sure you were ready."

Puzzled, she met his eyes questioningly. "Ready for what . . . ?"

"All the rest life has to offer, of course." Leaving her to ponder that for a moment, he caught the waiter's attention and indicated he wanted another Scotch before he said gently, "Your mother told me once how difficult it was for her to decide to marry someone outside the ballet world. Her own parents had endured so much to get out of Russia and make a life for themselves here. They were so proud of her talent, she was afraid she would be letting them down and betraying herself if she let anything but dance touch her."

Karla's eyes widened. Her hand shook slightly as she put her glass down. "But father and mother were deeply in love. How could she have even considered giving that up?"

"She didn't, once she realized her own feelings and your father's. They had ten joyful years together before she died and, when she was gone, you remained to fulfill the promise of everything they had shared."

27

"But I haven't," Karla was saying almost to herself. "All I've done is dance."

"And it's been enough, so far. But now—perhaps—it's time for something more."

She stared at him warily. To hear her most private thoughts spoken out loud by someone else, even so close a friend, was unnerving. Was she as transparent as that?

"Karla," Brad said gently, "I'd be the last person in the world to try to pressure you in any way. But you are a young, beautiful woman with an enormous amount to give. Sooner or later, dance may not be enough."

She managed to smile with far greater lightheartedness than she felt. "Sooner or later, *I* may not be enough. A ballerina's career is never long."

He brushed that aside. "You've already established yourself as a respected choreographer. One way or another, your career is secure. The question is, what about the other parts of your life?"

"There aren't any."

"Exactly my point."

When she did not respond to that, he tactfully let the subject go, for the moment. The conversation moved on to mutual friends, his business dealings, the ballet she was preparing. Dinner passed more swiftly than Karla would have liked.

As they stood outside under the awning, a crisp autumn wind swirled around them. It was dark, and all the lights of the city were on. New York was at its best: washed clean and invigorated by the new season.

"Autumn's my favorite time," Brad said as held

out a hand to help her into the long, black limousine that had appeared before them. "Always has been."

"Is that why you bought a football team?" Karla asked teasingly. "So you'd have an excuse to be outside on days like this?"

"Well, if I bought it as a business investment, I sure was in for a disappointment," he muttered. He broke off to remind the chauffeur that they would be dropping her at City Center. When he leaned back against the plush leather upholstery, he lit a thin cigar before unexpectedly asking, "Did you tell me the truth, about it going all right today?"

"Of course I did."

"Then you and Mac must have hit it off."

Karla glanced at him warily, surprised by the sudden mention of the man who had hovered at the edge of her thoughts ever since that morning. "What makes you say that?"

"Because he's the key to the whole team. The other men respect him enormously. Convince him that your program is worthwhile, and he'll bring the rest of them into line."

"And if he isn't convinced?"

"Then there will be problems. But if he gives you any trouble, you just tell me. I do have a little leverage with the great Mac Gregor."

"I should hope so," she murmured, "since you own the team."

Brad grinned self-deprecatingly. "Oh, that doesn't make any difference to Mac. He knows with his skills he could go anywhere. No, the only reason he might be inclined to listen to me is that we've developed mutual plans for his future he finds quite agreeable."

Despite herself, she could not quite contain her

curiosity enough to refrain from asking, "What plans?"

"Now, now, Karla. You don't go into great detail about a ballet before it's completely ready, do you?" She shook her head abashedly. "Well, I feel the same way about this arrangement with Mac. It has to remain private until he's absolutely convinced it's what he wants."

They had reached City Center where her choreography meeting was scheduled. Sliding out of the car ahead of the chauffeur, Brad held out a hand for her. Standing side by side on the curb, he dropped a gentle kiss on her cheek. "Give my boys hell, honey. They deserve it!"

She grinned up at him. "I'll do my best. Just remember when they come complaining that this was all your idea."

As he got back in the limo and it pulled away, she heard him laughing, a rich, full sound that oddly enough reminded her of another man's voice.

Mac Gregor was still on her mind hours later when she finally left the choreography meeting and stood on the darkened sidewalk outside City Center, trying to get up the energy to make her way back to her West Side apartment.

The new ballet was coming along very well. She should have felt satisfied and content. Instead, she had difficulty thinking about anything except a pair of remarkable sherry eyes and a perfect male body that combined virile strength with astounding gentleness.

Grimacing, she pulled her jacket more snugly around her and started walking. She really had to get control of herself. She was acting like an infatuated schoolgirl.

That struck her as funny. Her school years had been a whirlwind of juggling ballet lessons with academics, the latter usually getting the short end of the stick. Somehow, almost despite herself, she had managed to acquire a good education. But she had never, not once, experienced anything close to a schoolgirl crush.

She was kidding herself to think that that was what was happening now. The feelings Mac provoked in her were those of a full-grown woman.

Wryly, she shook her head. She had met him little more than twelve hours before, they had spent barely an hour together in the presence of some twenty-three other men, and they had exchanged only a handful of words, none of them private. Yet for all that, she couldn't get him out of her mind.

So firmly entrenched was he in her thoughts that for once she forgot her usual caution as she began walking down the dark street. When a shape suddenly loomed up beside her, her heart leaped into her throat. Jerking around, she fought down terrifying visions of the crimes routinely committed in the city as she confronted . . .

Mac? He stood before her, a figure out of her imagination, yet almost unbearably real. His hands were burrowed into the pockets of the jeans that hugged his narrow hips and sinewy legs. A soft wool shirt spanned the width of his massive chest, and a corduroy jacket the same shade as his chestnut hair did nothing to detract from the breadth of his shoulders.

The sudden, unexpected delight she felt at seeing

him sparked her temper. Angrily, she said, "You scared the daylights out of me! What are you doing here?"

"Sorry," he said sheepishly. "I didn't mean to frighten you. I . . . uh . . . happened to be in the neighborhood and thought you might want a lift." He nodded back toward the black Jaguar parked at the curb.

Karla stared up at him skeptically. "You happened to be?"

"Brad did mention where you were when we talked this evening," he admitted, taking her arm and unobtrusively steering her toward the car. More sternly, he added, "You really shouldn't be out by yourself at this hour. It isn't safe."

"No," she muttered as he gently but firmly eased her into the passenger seat. "I might be accosted by a pushy quarterback."

Sliding behind the wheel, Mac laughed. "There's no reason for you to worry about that. After all, this morning you stood up to an entire team without blinking."

His good humor was infectious. Forgetting her resentment at his sudden appearance, Karla said, "Shows what you know. I was shaking the whole time."

He cast her a surprised look as he maneuvered into traffic. Even at that hour, the streets were filled with late diners, daring tourists, and the night workers just starting their day.

It really was true, Karla mused, that New York never slept. At three o'clock in the morning, people would still be hurrying about looking for a taxi, a movie, a bagel. . . .

"Do you like bagels?" she asked suddenly.

"Love them, but what brought that on?"

"They're my big vice. I just got a terrible craving for one."

"Nobody can eat just one bagel," he scoffed.

"I can."

"This I have to see." Before she could stop him, he had pulled the Jaguar up outside an all-night bakery on Broadway renowned for its superb bagels. Jumping out, he said, "Stay there and protect the car. I'll be right back."

When he returned with a bag from which delicious aromas escaped, Karla exclaimed, "I didn't mean for you to do that, honestly. I was just—"

"Dreaming?"

She laughed self-consciously. "I guess so. I really can't afford to eat anything like that."

"Don't dancers burn up a lot of calories?"

"Sure, but that's no reason to get careless."

"I'll bet," he said with deceptive softness, "that you've never been careless in your life."

Something in his tone stung her. He seemed to be repudiating the discipline that was an essential part of her profession. Tartly, she said, "Oh, I don't know about that. After all, I got in the car, didn't I?"

There was a moment's silence, during which she glanced uneasily at Mac. A little sigh of relief escaped her as she saw that he was grinning broadly.

"Touché. I deserved that." Taking his eyes from the road for just an instant, he murmured, "You don't take any nonsense, do you?"

"No more than you, I'd guess."

"Sounds like we're two of a kind."

She couldn't help but laugh at that, though there

was very little humor in it. "Hardly. We come from completely different worlds."

He glanced at her again, the light from the street-lamps reflecting off his burnished skin and casting the rough-hewn bones of his face into sharp prominence. "How do you figure that?"

"It should be obvious. Ballet and football don't exactly attract the same kind of people."

"Brad's a fan of both. He's told me how magnificently you dance."

The knowledge that the two men had talked about her surprised and distressed her, even though she told herself there had been a good reason for it. "I suppose you were talking about the exercise program for the team?"

"No," Mac said shortly, "we were talking about you."

She shot him a quick look. "Why?"

Instead of answering directly, he said, "Brad cares a great deal about you, doesn't he?"

"Yes," Karla admitted, more bewildered than ever. What was he leading up to? "He's been like a father to me since my dad died."

"He told me about that. I'm sorry."

She silently accepted his sympathy, surprised by its obvious sincerity. After a moment he said, "You and I do have something in common then, despite what you thought." At her puzzled look, he grinned. "Brad tends to treat me like an adopted son, worrying about my health, my future, and so on. You probably don't know it, but he's responsible for my career in football."

"He never told me that."

"No, he doesn't like to talk about that side of

34

himself, the part that really cares about people. It makes him self-conscious. But the fact remains, if he hadn't encouraged me, I'd never have made it this far."

"Why not?" Karla asked softly. She sensed she was about to hear something Mac didn't share with many people, and the knowledge that he was willing to open up to her so much touched her deeply

His hands tightened on the wheel as he said, "I was twenty-one when I turned pro, straight out of college. I thought I was the hottest thing on two feet, and I set out to prove it." He sighed into the darkness. "Hell, I was a kid out of the West Virginia coal mines. Nobody in my family ever had much more than a dime to call his own. All of a sudden there was money, fame, women . . . It went to my head in the worst way."

"You can hardly be blamed for that."

"No? I came pretty close to betraying a lot of people's faith in me. I started missing practice, screwing up on the field, letting the team down. By the end of my first season, I'd been cut from the squad and was on a one-way slide to nowhere. That's when Brad got involved."

"He talked some sense into you?"

Mac laughed sardonically. "*Pounded* would be more accurate. He got me up to his fishing camp in the Rockies and really let loose. Read me the riot act on how I was throwing away a chance plenty of guys my age would kill for. Then he put me to work in one of his lumber camps. I spent six months there. Six *tough* months. When they were over, he gave me a choice: Go back to the mines and spend my life the way every other man in my family had or try again for a chance at something better."

He paused a moment before he said softly, "The second time around I didn't blow it, thanks to Brad. That was twelve years ago. Now I'm getting close to the end of a terrific career, and I know I owe it all to him."

"Brad would be the first person to tell you that isn't true. You owe it to yourself, your talent, ambition, drive. He just helped along the way."

Sherry eyes grinned at her. "You've heard that speech, too, right?"

She couldn't help but blush. His perception was disconcerting. Why had she believed only artistic types were capable of seeing into another person's innermost thoughts?

"Brad pulled me through a rough time after Dad died," she explained. "I was at the most crucial point in my career, and the pressure combined with grief was just too much." Grimly she recalled, "I fell apart on stage one night and afterward I was convinced I could never dance in public again." A dry smile curved her lips as she said, "I spent my time at his place in the Rockies, too. Although I have to admit, Brad never found it necessary to send me to any lumber camp."

"Good thing," Mac growled. "You would have made mincemeat of a perfectly good crew."

Surprised, she said the first thing that came into her head. "Is that what you think I'm doing to your team?"

"All I know is that after you left today, there was more than a little moaning and groaning."

"Not from you, though," she teased. "You were just warmed up."

"Oh, I'm warmed up all right," he informed her, a caressing note in his voice, which made her stiffen at the same time that her insides coiled deliciously.

"Mac, there's something we should get straight right away."

"What's that?" he asked mildly as he parked the Jag in front of her brownstone.

"How did you know where I lived?" she asked, forgetting for an instant what she had meant to say.

"*That's* what we need to get straight?"

"No, of course not. I just want to know."

He sighed exaggeratedly as he helped her out of the low-slung sports car. "Brad told me."

Karla's eyes flashed. "I see. Is there anything else he found necessary to mention?"

"Yep."

"Well . . . ?"

"I'll tell you upstairs." He leaned forward, touching the tip of her nose lightly. "Provided you toast the bagels."

"Mac, I never meant for you to come up with me."

He pretended to look dismayed. "You don't really mean to turn a man away from such incredible temptation." At her censorious frown, he pointed to the bag she held. "The bagels, of course. What did you think I meant?"

"Nothing! It's just that . . ."

The teasing faded from his eyes. Taking hold of her shoulders gently, he met her wary gaze calmly as he said, "I'm harmless, Karla. Believe me."

She didn't. Mac Gregor was about as harmless as a playful grizzly bear. He would grab anything he wanted and, more likely than not, rip it to shreds in the process.

Or would he? She still couldn't shake the memory of the concern she had glimpsed in him when he thought she wouldn't be able to stand up to the players.

He had intervened on her behalf and been ready to do it again even after she rebuffed his overtures. Perhaps that was the West Virginian in him. She had heard that mountain men were rough but gallant.

The disarming innocence in his eyes won out, even over her common sense. "Oh, all right. It'll be worth it, if only to prove to you that I can so eat only one bagel."

He was still smiling as the trooped up the three flights of stairs to her top-floor apartment and she fumbled with her keys to open the door. On impulse, she thought it necessary to warn him, "It's not much. I've never really gotten around to decorating."

"That's okay," he assured her gently. "I hired a guy to do my place. He turned it into his idea of how a pro quarterback should live." A grimace twisted his mouth. "I'm not crazy about it."

"Then maybe you'll like this better," Karla said more confidently, easing open the door. "It's definitely not glamorous."

That was an understatement. Her studio apartment with its small kitchen and bath was clean and larger than many similar accommodations in New York. It even boasted such amenities as a high ceiling, large windows, a fireplace, and two closets. But as far as furniture went . . .

Her platform bed occupied a good chunk of the available space. It was king-size for no better reason than the fact that it had seemed a good idea when she bought it.

Behind the bed, built-in bookcases held her collection of reference works about dance. A bright, hand-made quilt picked up the same vivid blues and reds and greens as the large pillows scattered in front of the fireplace.

That was it. Tables, chairs, couches were all just so much clutter she could do without. Her only concession to non-necessities was a large vase of fresh roses, her favorite flower and a luxury she gave herself regularly. Just then, as Mac glanced around, she wished she had paid a little more attention to a few other social niceties.

"Uh . . . it's very nice," he began. "Spacious . . ."

"Don't you mean bare?" she inquired softly.

"Karla"—he hesitated, looking around again before facing her squarely—"how much do dancers make?"

"W-what?"

"I mean, I thought you were doing pretty well. But if you can't even afford furniture—"

A laugh she couldn't suppress bubbled to the surface. "Mac, I hate to spoil this for you, but I do very nicely, thank you. It's true most dancers have it tough financially, but I've been lucky enough to make it to the top ranks where the pay is as good as it is for stars in any other business. I've just never been inclined to own a lot of things."

"How come?" he asked, following her into the kitchen as she rummaged around for a knife with which to slice the bagels. "I don't mean to pry, you understand. I'm just curious."

"That's all right. I know you mean well. I guess I've been too busy to care. As long as I had a roof over my head and a bed to fall into at night, I didn't need anything else."

She turned toward him, only to stop as she realized how close they were standing. The kitchen was small enough for one person; when there were two, and one of those was very tall and broad, the space shrunk to claustrophobic proportions.

"Uh . . excuse me, I need to get that pan."

"Oh, sure, sorry." Stepping out of her way, he watched as she spread the bagels on a flat cookie sheet and popped them under the broiler.

"They'll only take a few minutes," she said when she found him watching her. "I see you remembered the cream cheese."

"What're bagels without cream cheese? Now if only we had some lox—"

"Please. You're corrupting me enough as it is."

Despite the humor evident in her voice, he shook his head ruefully. "You must lead an incredibly pure life if a few bagels are really your idea of vice."

"One bagel," she reminded him, ignoring the thought of what he would think if he knew exactly how pure her life really was. He probably wouldn't believe her, not coming from the world he did.

"Does your fireplace work?" he asked as they gathered up knives and plates and carried them back into the living room.

"As far as I know. I haven't used it since last winter."

"Mind if I give it a try?"

Karla could think of few things she would enjoy more than sharing a roaring fire with such a compelling man. But then she supposed that just went to show how very innocent she was.

Mac could undoubtedly think of quite a few more enjoyable pursuits. The trick was going to be getting him out of her apartment before he tried to involve her in any of them.

Somehow she lost track of that once they were settled in front of the cheerful fire, munching on bagels and sharing a bottle of Beaujolais she had unearthed from a cabinet.

"Not bad," Mac allowed as he finished his second glass. "But I'll have to bring some beer over here." He glanced around again, his eyes teasing. "Couple of chairs wouldn't hurt, either."

Nodding his head firmly, as though having reached some decision, he announced, "Yep, what this place definitely needs is a man's touch."

Karla couldn't help but laugh. "Beer cans and big armchairs?"

"Not bad for a start. A few clothes scattered around, last Sunday's sports section, a few smelly pipes . . . you'd be all set."

"Somehow I get the feeling you're not much more domesticated than I am."

"Nope," he agreed readily. Sherry eyes caught hers as he added softly, "Looks to me as though we're a couple of strays looking for a home."

Karla shifted uneasily. Her unusually full stomach and the wine she had drunk were making her feel dangerously content. It would be very easy to give herself up to the spell the man before her wove so effortlessly.

Cautiously she said, "I already have a home, Mac. The ballet."

41

"Do you really believe that?" he asked softly. Sitting in front of the fire with his jacket off and his long, taut body gracefully at rest, he looked like a proud, free animal filled with strength and spirit. Yet his manner was gentle, as though he was somehow well aware of her vulnerability, and determined not to hurt her.

"Of course I believe it," Karla murmured huskily, not noticing that she had put her glass down and moved slightly closer to him. She felt very warm. The wool sweater and skirt that had seemed well suited to the crisp day were suddenly almost suffocating.

She wanted . . . what? The caress of silk against her skin . . . the sense of exhilaration that seized her when she danced but which she had never known at any other time . . . the touch of the big, powerful hands that had held her so carefully . . .

"Ballet," Mac said huskily, bending toward her, "isn't any more of a home than football. Don't you ever want more? One special person who cares for you more than anything else in the world?"

Her indigo eyes opened wider behind thick lashes. "Is that how you think of home?"

He nodded slowly, raising a hand to gently brush against the delicate curve of her cheek. "It isn't a place or a collection of things. It's a feeling of rightness, belonging. A haven safe from all the rest of the world."

Karla swallowed with some difficulty. The touch of his fingers against her skin was wreaking havoc with her emotions. Distractedly, she moistened her lips, startled by the sudden flaring of Mac's nostrils.

Raggedly he murmured, "Would you let me do

something I've been wanting to do ever since I first saw you?"

She thought he meant to kiss her and found that suddenly she wanted that, too. Very much. Mutely, she nodded.

But Mac surprised her. Raising both hands, he reached behind her for the heavy weight of her braid. Deftly, with skill that surprised her, he undid it and combed the strands free with his fingers.

"Like silk," he murmured when her ebony hair lay loosely about her shoulders. "Dark, midnight silk."

"Y-you don't sound like a football player," she whispered, hardly aware of what she was saying.

"Forget that part of me," he rasped. "I'm a man, that's all."

That was enough, she thought dimly as his head moved slowly down toward her. *Oh, lord, it was more than enough.* She was drowning in feeling, hardly able to breathe, and he hadn't even kissed her yet!

When he did, the sensation was unlike anything else she had ever experienced. Not even the soaring ecstasy of the prima ballerina's solo in *Swan Lake* or the aching beauty of the pas de deux in *Romeo and Juliet* had prepared her for what she experienced.

At first, his touch was feather-light, his lips barely brushing hers. At her tentative yet unmistakable response, he groaned softly. "God, Karla, you're so lovely. So strong, yet so feminine. Let me . . ."

No thought of refusal remained in her mind as he tenderly lowered her to the floor in front of the fireplace, his steely arms reaching around to protect her from the hard surface.

A piercing sense of being cherished swept over her. Never in her life had she felt like this. Mac touched her as though she were infinitely precious and, in doing so, made her believe it was true.

His big, hard body bent over her, his mouth seeking hers with gentle, persuasive nibbles that made her yearn for more. When his tongue darted out to trace the ridge of her teeth, she couldn't hold back a low moan of delight. Her slender, finely honed body arched against his strength . . . seeking, wanting . . .

Without being aware that she did so, she dug her fingers into his broad shoulders, savoring the taut power of muscle and sinew. He felt so good.

When he picked her up and crossed the room in rapid strides to deposit her on the bed, she offered no demur. Nothing could make her stop this magic. Her slender arms were wrapped around his neck, her lips clinging to his, as they fell together across the wide mattress.

As their tongues met and dueled erotically, Mac's large, warm hands moved down the line of her body, lingering on the high, firm curve of her breasts, her small waist, the rounded promise of her hips. By the time he found her slim, taut thighs he was trembling with need.

"Karla, my God, you're so beautiful . . . exquisite . . ." A low growl broke from him as his tongue thrust deeply, plundering the sweet moistness of her mouth.

Even in the midst of desire so great that she could feel it reverberating through him, he moved with immense caution. Holding his weight off her, he trailed gentle kisses down the vulnerable line of her throat to the hollow at its base. There his lips sipped thirstily through endless moments before she at last cried out softly.

"Mac, please, you make me feel—"

He raised his head, sherry eyes dark with ancient fire. "What, darling? What do I make you feel?"

"So much . . . I don't know, it's all so new . . ."

He smiled at first. Then slowly, his masculine pleasure gave way to faint concern. Moving off her slightly, despite her efforts to stop him, he gazed down at her closely.

"Karla, have you had much experience with men?"

Her eyes widened, meeting his with surprise. What a thing to ask at such a time! How could she answer him? Already she sensed his doubt and, without questioning why, wanted desperately to erase it.

"N-not much." That wasn't completely true, but close enough that she hoped he would be satisfied. Raising her hands, she caressed the rugged planes of his face as she lifted herself slightly, enough to bring her breasts into contact with his steely chest. "It doesn't matter, does it?"

Mac hesitated. He couldn't remember the last time he had wanted a woman so desperately. His body was on fire with need for her. Yet something stopped him from giving vent to the powerful urges she unleashed.

"Yes," he muttered shakily. "I think it just might." Gently, determined not to hurt her in any way, he disentangled himself and sat up. Passing a shaky hand through his tousled hair, he looked down at her tenderly.

I must be out of my mind. When had a woman

looked lovelier or more desirable? Her cheeks were flushed, her eyes glowing with passion equal to his own. Her soft, delectable lips were slightly parted, inviting his further exploration.

His gaze drifted lower. Through the thin wool of her sweater, he could clearly see the outline of her firm breasts and taut nipples. He swallowed hard and met her eyes again. She was gazing at him with mingled innocence and concern, her expression mirroring the tumult of her mind and spirit.

At that moment he knew that all he wanted in the world lay before him, his for the taking. He had only to reach out. Yet he could not.

An instinct, both protective and prudent, warned that it was too soon. If he took her now, they would both regret it.

Even as his body raged at him, the strong will that had carried him to the apex of his career took command. He stood up, lifted her hand to his lips, and kissed the open palm gently. Huskily, he breathed, "I'll see you tomorrow."

The murmured words barely pierced the wall of Karla's shock. She watched in disbelief as Mac walked away, quietly closing the door behind him.

CHAPTER THREE

Karla reluctantly climbed out of bed the next morning. She wanted nothing so much as to stay right where she was, hidden under the covers and protected from the world.

But it wasn't to be. She had responsibilities . . . and pride. No matter how bewildered she was by Mac's behavior, she had no choice but to face him.

Long hours of lying awake wondering why he had departed so abruptly had left their mark. Staring at her unusually pale reflection in the bathroom mirror, she saw lavender shadows beneath her eyes.

Silently cursing both herself and him, she stood under the shower for long moments, hoping to inject some sense of energy into her limp body. As she was drying off, she stared down at herself critically.

What she saw didn't look too bad. Granted, her breasts were smallish, but that was to be expected of a dancer. Rigorous training strengthened the pectoral muscles and led inevitably to a high, firm bosom.

Her waist was pleasantly slender and her hips, though slim, were definitely rounded.

Cleaning steam off the mirror, she frowned. If he wasn't attracted to her, why had he kissed her in the first place?

Good question. Unfortunately, she lacked an answer. Mac's motives were as much a mystery as her own. She had never intended to let him come upstairs with her, never intended to let down her guard so drastically, to . . .

To almost make love with him. Honesty forced her to admit that was what would have happened if he hadn't stopped when he did.

Why hadn't he taken advantage of her obvious susceptibility?

Over a breakfast of cereal sprinkled with wheat germ and a small glass of grapefruit juice, she recalled the glimmer of something very much like regret in his eyes just before he walked away.

Perhaps she was just kidding herself, but it almost seemed as though he had been waging a battle within himself, one he had come close to losing. That possibility at least enabled her to dress and make the trip to the Flyers' stadium with the appearance of calm.

The day, like its predecessor, was crisp and clear. A cobalt blue sky hung above the city, for once free of the miasma of pollution that too often layered the air. There were only the bright hues of autumn in evidence as she turned her small car into the parking lot and slid into one of the reserved spaces near the entrance.

A security guard nodded to her as she walked up the ramp and through the chainlink gate. Once inside, she headed straight for the exercise room.

Down on the field she could make out the specialty teams going through their drills.

The sound of deep, male voices and the solid thump of powerful bodies striking each other filled the air. Tempted to pause, she kept moving. If Mac was there, she didn't want to see him. At least not yet.

In the private locker room, she hung up her mustard yellow coat and removed the navy blue skirt she wore over a burgundy leotard and tights. Surveying herself in the mirror, she pinned her hair up in a neat chignon before slipping into her pointe shoes.

At the bar, she went through a few quick exercises to limber up. By the time she had completed a series of pliés, battements, rélevés, and coupés, she felt more like herself and better able to face whatever might be ahead.

Sounds from the next room alerted her to the fact that the men were trailing in. She thought she could detect a notable lack of enthusiasm in their muted voices. Her plans about how she would conduct this class seemed wiser than ever.

By the time the first players began to straggle in, the projector and screen she had requested were in place. Greeting the men by name, she was gratified by a few semicourteous nods and curious glances at the equipment.

When the last group arrived, Mac among them, she immediately asked for the lights to be turned off and directed their attention to the screen. The diversion gave her an opportunity not to look at the man who had so dominated her thoughts ever since she woke from an uneasy sleep.

But she was still vividly aware of his eyes on her

as the film began to roll. Not even the magnificent, explosive form of Edward Villella could command her attention completely. Stripped to the waist, his burnished torso ridged with muscle and sinew and his powerful arms taut with barely leashed power, the renowned dancer was the epitome of male grace and virility.

She was only half-aware of the superb performance going on across the screen until the indrawn breaths of the astonished men, many of whom had never seen a ballet, reminded her of its importance to her plan.

"Yesterday," she said quietly, "I got the impression that some of you believe ballet is for sissies. So I thought you might like to see what a man can do with dance."

Conscious now of the eyes riveted on the screen, she went on, "Edward Villella is one of the greatest dancers in history. He brought a level of power and virility to the ballet that has rarely been seen before or since. You may be interested to know that he's married, has two children, and has taught ballet classes at West Point, for exactly the same purpose I'm here to teach you."

Smiling slightly, she wound up what looked to be a successful sales pitch. "Now some of you may still believe only effeminate men dance. But I wouldn't advise you to tell Villella that. I think you'll agree he's a match for any of you."

This was met by reluctant chuckles and nods of assent as the lights went back on. There was a new ease about the men that was gratifying to see. Karla didn't kid herself that the battle was completely won, but at least she had made some progress.

Winning the men over proved to be the least of her problems as she began putting them through a series of exercises similar to what they had done the day before, but slightly more demanding. Try though she did to concentrate on the group as a whole, she could not escape her vivid awareness of Mac. He was watching her intently, his eyes hooded so that she could not guess what was in his mind. Nor did he join in the usual bantering or wry complaints.

Only once did he lose the careful self-containment he had maintained since he'd come into the room and been met by her determined coolness. When one of the players began to comment on her appearance in terms that would have been flattering had they not been accompanied by a nasty leer, Mac suddenly stiffened.

"That's enough, Mullaney," he ordered harshly. "Keep your mind on what you're supposed to be doing."

Startled by the anger he made no effort to hide, the men looked from her to Mac in dawning comprehension. Barely a moment passed before the class resumed, but it was enough to change the mood in the room.

By going to her defense so unequivocally, Mac had stamped her as his own and as good as told every other man there to stay away from her. Karla didn't know whether to be pleased or angered by his behavior.

On the one hand, she told herself he had no right to behave so high-handedly. She was a grown woman who could fight her own battles. But she couldn't deny that some fundamentally feminine part of herself responded to his protection.

The reminder of how easily he could make her behave in ways alien to her character stiffened her resolve to hide her emotions from him. As the class ended, she was glad of the half dozen or so players who stopped to chat.

Recognizing their questions as a bid for, if not friendship, at least accord, she responded patiently to each. In doing so, she had an ulterior motive. Surely by the time she was finished, Mac would be long gone?

He wasn't. When the last player took himself off, he was still standing off to one side, watching her. His arms were folded over his powerful chest, his feet planted slightly apart.

Once again, she was struck by the sensation of being looked after. Wryly she had to admit that this time, at least, he'd been a little less obtrusive about it.

He met her mildly chagrined gaze calmly. Not the sweat streaking his rugged features or the gray work-suit he wore could detract from his compelling virility. Karla swallowed tightly, struggling to beat down the traitorous feelings that threatened to claim her.

All too vividly she recalled the previous evening when he had so effortlessly swept away her innate restraint and come perilously close to claiming her completely.

Sternly she told herself she couldn't afford to be so susceptible to any man, much less one from a completely different world, who could walk away from her without a backward glance.

"Was there something you wanted?" she asked, struggling for a faintly censorious tone that would suggest he was keeping her from something more important.

A rueful smile lit his eyes. "Yes, but this is hardly the time or place." At her swift blush, he laughed. "My second choice is to talk." Letting his arms drop to his sides, he took a step closer. "What's wrong, Karla? Since I walked in here, you've been doing your damnedest to pretend I don't exist."

"Don't be silly," she protested, instinctively moving backward before she caught herself and stopped. "I've been very busy. Teaching a class of twenty-four reluctant beginners isn't easy."

"No, but you've already worked wonders. Showing that film was a great idea."

"Thanks. Now if there's nothing else—"

"Hold on. Of course there is." He frowned, taking in the pallor of her hollowed cheeks and the shadows beneath her eyes. "What's happened to you since yesterday?"

Karla's eyes widened. He had to be kidding. Didn't he realize the effect he had on her?

Perhaps not, because he was staring at her with what looked for all the world like genuine bewilderment. Hesitantly, he asked, "You're not . . . embarrassed, are you?"

I only wish I was! Instead, all she could manage was regret that their lovemaking had not reached its natural conclusion. Not for the world would she admit that to him.

"Of course not. Why would I be?"

"No reason. I just thought maybe . . . Never mind."

"If that's all then—" She started moving toward the door.

"No!" Just as it had the previous day, his hand lashed out to take hold of her, stopping her from retreating. Startled, she stared at him in dismay.

Dark color stained his prominent cheekbones as he instantly dropped her arm. "I'm sorry," he murmured. "I keep grabbing you, and I honestly don't mean to. It's just that—"

"That what?" she asked, hardly aware that she did so. All her attention was focused on the genuine regret and—fear?—she saw in his eyes.

"That you're so different from anyone I've ever known," he admitted reluctantly. "I'm not quite sure you're real. I keep thinking that if I don't do something to stop you, you'll drift away from me."

Surprised by the unexpected glimpse he had given her of his own insecurities, Karla softened. Against her better judgment, in obedience to some instinct she didn't want to examine too closely, she said, "I think we'd better talk, Mac. This verbal fencing we seem to be doing won't get us anywhere."

He nodded, clearly surprised by her candor. "I'll wait for you outside while you change." She could hear the relief in his voice.

The image of him slouched against the door of the exercise room, once again warning away all others, made her laugh. The day was suddenly far brighter than she would have thought possible. Too wise to question such unexpected pleasure, she cast him a teasing look.

"I think you'd better change, too. That outfit doesn't look like it would wear too well outside the locker room."

Glancing down at himself he grinned. "You're right. The only place I could take you dressed like this is some jock bar, and I've got no intention of doing that."

The look he gave her made it clear why not. Shaking his head, he muttered, "Isn't there something you could wear besides those skimpy leotards?"

About to enter her changing room, she glanced over her shoulder at him. "Nope, you'll just have to keep the guys in line."

"Oh, believe me, I will," he assured her as she let the door swing shut between them.

Humming softly to herself, Karla hurried through a quick shower before putting on her navy blue skirt paired with a persimmon-colored sweater. Stuffing her dancing gear into her bag, she let down her hair and brushed it briskly before tossing her coat over her arm and going to find Mac.

As promised, he was waiting in the corridor. The sweat suit was gone, replaced by perfectly tailored gray slacks and a cable-knit sweater in natural wool, which made his huge chest and shoulders look even more massive than ever. Chestnut hair shot through with sun-warmed strands of gold glinted damply.

In the unguarded moment before he saw her, his eyes were very somber, as though he were looking inward at something that left him concerned and hesitant.

That expression vanished the moment he caught sight of her. A warm, caressing smile softened his rough-hewn features. But it could not quite hide the vulnerability she had glimpsed briefly. That, more than anything else, made her greet him with the light touch of her lips against his burnished cheek.

Before he could respond, she said, "I have class in a couple of hours. We'll have to go somewhere fast."

"I know the perfect spot," he murmured, holding the outer door open for her. Watching the slight, uncontrived sway of her hips as she passed through, he added, "Let's leave my car here and take yours. I'll pick it up later."

Surprised, she nodded. She'd thought he would insist on doing the driving. Instead, he slipped into the passenger seat beside her without protest and was silent as she maneuvered the compact into traffic.

Not until they were heading into the city on one of the broad ribbons of highway that intersected periodically like woven strands of taffy did he speak again.

"Karla, I'm sorry if I upset you last night. After I left, I realized it must have seemed very abrupt to you, my just walking out like that. But I had the best of motives, believe me."

She was inclined to, if only because he looked so genuinely contrite. "I think I've managed to figure that out. Of course, it took me a while." Casting him a sidelong glance, she added softly, "Mac, I think the problem is that we've gotten a bit ahead of ourselves. We really don't know each other well at all and, coming from such different worlds as we do, any presumptions we make are liable to be wrong. Both of us could get hurt."

"I realize that," he said somberly. "That's what made me leave last night." He was silent for a moment before adding, "I don't know what it is about you, Karla, but I can't stand the idea of hurting you, even inadvertently. You're very different from the women I've known. In some ways you're much stronger and more self-reliant, but I also get the feeling that you can be very vulnerable."

"I won't even try to deny that. Sometimes I've wished I had a thicker skin, but if I did, I wouldn't be able to dance as well." Stopping at a red light, she turned to look at him. "Mac, I think we need to get to know each other as friends before we try for anything more."

"That's what I was thinking, but honestly I'm not sure how to go about it."

"Why's that?"

"I've never really been friends with a woman. I know that's a terrible admission to make nowadays, but it's the truth. Somehow, the opportunity just has never come up."

Admiring his honesty, even as she had to regret the narrowness of his experience, she said, "A lot of my friends are men, but that's to be expected in the ballet. When you sweat and hurt and dream together, you end up caring about each other."

"These friends of yours . . . are they . . . uh, interested in women?"

Karla bit down on the tip of her tongue to keep from laughing. He was trying so hard to be broadminded; the fact that he wasn't succeeding entirely didn't seem too important. "Some are and some aren't."

"And you're really telling me that a man who, uh, is interested in women can be friends with a woman without anything else being involved?" he asked doubtfully.

"Yes, although sometimes such friendships do lead to more."

His face tightened slightly. "With you?"

"No, I've always been so busy . . . first climbing the rungs as a dancer and more recently as a choreographer. Right now, I juggle both jobs. That doesn't leave much time for anything else."

"But you're making time for us." That might have been a question; instead it was a clear-cut statement not simply of what was happening right then but also of how he saw the future. Whatever doubts he might have about his ability to build a friendship with a woman, they did not weaken his determination to go on seeing her.

"Because I don't seem to have any choice," Karla admitted dryly.

Mac glanced at her worriedly for a moment before his features cleared. She was referring not to his persistence, but to her own feelings, which she could not deny. "That's the best news I could get."

Tartly she advised, "Don't look so pleased with yourself. I meant what I said about getting to be friends first."

"Fine with me," he insisted. "Let's start out by having a friendly lunch."

His suggestion of a quiet, neighborhood restaurant on the West Side turned out to be excellent. It was a family-run place, sporting a bright red-and-white-striped awning out in front, along with boxes of late-blooming geraniums and white lace curtains in the windows.

The plump, matronly woman who bustled forward to greet them was introduced as Mrs. B. Mac put an arm around her ample waist and kissed her soundly on the cheek as she clucked over him.

"So where have you been these last couple of weeks? How do you expect to win if you don't eat right? All the time, go-go-go? What would your momma say?"

When he was finally able to get a word in edgewise, Mac said, "She'd thank you for looking after me so well, Mrs. B. You do such a good job, I even brought a friend to meet you." His hand on Karla's elbow urged her forward.

The older woman looked her up and down carefully before a wide grin split her cheerful face. "So finally you meet a decent woman. It's about time. You're not getting any younger. Come on, sit down, you'll eat something."

As Mac began to caution her on that score, she raised her hands heavenward. "I know, I know. You have to work out this afternoon. No wine, no dessert. Nothing heavy." Casting Karla a knowing look, Mrs. B. added, "Don't tell me you're the same. What are you, a model?"

"No, I'm a dancer."

"Karla's a ballerina, Mrs. B. And a choreographer. At City Center."

"I knew you were something special the minute I looked at you," their hostess assured her. "Every year I take my grandchildren to see *The Nutcracker.* Beautiful." Arranging glasses of mineral water, a basket of fresh-baked bread, and a dish of creamy butter in front of them, she asked, "You ever dance in that?"

"Yes, several years ago I was the Sugarplum Fairy."

"Oh, my favorite! Such a thrill. I never seen anything else like that in my life. Wait'll I tell the kids who was in here today."

"Won't they be glad to hear I dropped by?" Mac teased.

"You they can see anytime on television. But a real ballerina . . ." About to wax eloquent, Mrs. B. caught herself. Shaking her head, she said, "What am I thinking of? Two attractive young people come in here, they don't want to listen to me. Sit, look at the menu, talk. I'll be back later for your order."

The fond look she beamed at them prompted Mac to say teasingly, "Don't get the wrong idea. Karla and I are just friends."

Mrs. B. was not impressed. Hurrying off to the kitchen, she murmured, "Sure, sure. Even friends have to eat. Now where's that lasagna?"

"She's a character, but I love her," Mac said when they were alone at the table. "Since I moved to New York, she's been like a second mother to me."

"I'll bet she doesn't let you get away with anything," Karla kidded. She was dimly aware of the other diners around them, many of whom had recognized Mac and were watching them with interest. But in typical New York fashion, their attention was unobtrusive. It was a point of pride to always behave nonchalantly, even among the great and famous. More softly, she added, "Thank you for bringing me here."

"It's no big deal," Mac claimed in obvious contradiction of what the place so clearly meant to him. "It's just somewhere to eat."

Karla let that small deception go by. She had no doubt that his bringing her to Mrs. B's was a further sign that he viewed her differently from other women he had known. That knowledge warmed her and made a delicious meal all the more enjoyable.

Over endive salad, zucchini lasagna, and espresso

flavored with twists of lemon peel, they began to discover more about each other.

Mac told her about his childhood in West Virginia, about growing up in a small, crowded house on the edge of the mines where the air was never quite clean, clothes were always at least a little grimy, and money was ever in short supply.

"My two older brothers worked in the mines to get through college. I was lucky enough to have a football scholarship. Tad, he's the lawyer, got hurt in an accident the summer he was twenty. He still walks with a limp. Funny thing, all through high school he was a better player than I was. Could have gone the same route I did, before he was injured."

"What stopped him?"

"A woman. Girl, really. She talked him out of applying to college, wanted him to stay home and marry her. Turned out she'd gotten knocked up . . . uh, pregnant by some other guy. By the time Tad found out, it was too late for that scholarship. He didn't wind up marrying her, but he did wind up in the mines."

"But he got out, anyway."

"Once he made up his mind there was no stopping him." Mac grinned unabashedly. "All the Gregor men are very inwardly directed. Which is a fancy way of saying we see what we want and go for it."

"I've noticed," Karla murmured, flushing slightly under his scrutiny. "Was your brother very bitter about what the girl did?"

"For a while, but he got over it. I wouldn't be surprised if he takes the plunge pretty soon."

"Plunge?"

61

"Gets married. He's met somebody who seems good for him, and vice versa."

A sudden thought occurred to Karla. Putting down her glass, she asked, "Have you ever been married?"

Mac laughed and shook his head. "Not me. I've never even come close."

"A girl in every town?" she asked dryly, pretending a casualness she did not feel.

"Not quite, but enough to make it clear I had no intention of getting serious."

"Did you like that life?"

"I'd be a liar if I said otherwise. But lately . . ." He shrugged lightly. "Enough about me. Let's see what I know about you."

Holding up a large, capable hand, he ticked off his fingers. "Your father was a marine but you somehow ended up as a ballerina. You've danced almost all your life. More recently you've become a choreographer. You're fantastic at both, the toast of seven continents. 'The Steel Butterfly,' they call you. While you've built your career, you've had no time or inclination for personal entanglements. Am I right so far?"

Karla nodded reluctantly. "I don't remember telling you so much."

"You didn't, not all of it, anyway. Brad filled in some of the blanks."

"You never did tell me what else he said when you talked yesterday."

Mac leaned back in his chair and studied her thoughtfully. Quietly he said, "He told me even steel butterflies could get dented and that if I hurt you,

62

there wouldn't be a safe place on earth for me to hide."

Across the table littered with the remains of lunch, they stared at each other. In his deep-set eyes shot through with golden glints she saw an unspoken promise. He would be careful and go slowly with her. But in the end she would still be his.

CHAPTER FOUR

"You're going to love this," Brad assured her as he ushered Karla into his private box overlooking the field. "You've got the best view in the house, right smack on the fifty-yard line. Not to mention the best escort." Grinning boyishly, he gestured to the uniformed steward who hurried forward.

"I feel lucky today," Brad said. "How about a bottle of bubbly?"

"The Tattinger, sir?"

"The very one, very dry and very cold. How does that sound to you, sweetheart?"

"Extravagant," Karla assured him wryly. "But never let it be said I turned down champagne."

"Good girl. Got anything to go with that?"

"A rather nice pâté, sir, as well as a selection of cheeses and fresh fruit."

Brad nodded his approval as he ushered Karla into one of the plush leather armchairs overlooking the field, and settled himself beside her. Protected by a plate glass window, the private box was a world away from the bleacher seats where the fans were gathering. The crowd seemed impressive to her, but he quickly dissuaded her of that notion.

"Attendance is lousy so far this year, but who can blame the public for staying away? No one wants to watch losers."

"I thought everyone agreed the Flyers were a fine team that had just had a run of bad luck."

"That's true, we've had more than our share of injuries. But this is still a win-or-lose proposition. Nobody gets points for meaning well or trying hard."

"Then it isn't how you play the game that counts?" she asked a bit grimly.

"No way! Football is big business. Sale of television rights alone amounts to millions of dollars every year. Teams get bonuses for making it into the playoffs, and everyone hopes to reach the Super Bowl."

At her tight-lipped look, he laughed. "It isn't all bad. We try to maintain a much stricter code of ethics than just about any other business, partly because we're so much in the public eye, but also because a lot of kids emulate their favorite players. If they see a guy taking it easy on the field, letting down the team, they think that's okay. Without belaboring the point, we make an effort to set a good example."

"That's why players like Mac spend so much time with youngsters?"

Brad cast her a sharp glance. "How did you know about that?"

"I read an article about him in one of the newsmagazines." She didn't add that she had come across it the previous night when, unable to sleep, she had tried unsuccessfully to find some way to stop thinking about Mac.

They hadn't seen each other since the lunch at Mrs. B's. He'd had to go back to the stadium for practice while she went to class. The usual pre-game curfew kept him from taking her to dinner that evening.

When Brad called with the invitation to the game, Karla had jumped at it eagerly. She told herself she just wanted to get better acquainted with the players she was supposed to be helping. And that was part of it. But she wasn't about to turn down a chance to see Mac again, even at a distance.

"He's a great guy," Brad was saying. "One of the all-time best. When you look at the records he's set, it's amazing that he's never played on a championship team." Sighing, he added, "I'd hoped he might have one more shot at it, but if the Flyers' performance so far this year is anything to go by, we'll barely make it through the season."

"Why is that?" Karla asked, accepting a glass of champagne from the steward.

"The main problem is that we have a lot of new players who haven't worked together as a unit before. They're as sharp and talented as you could ask for, but they've got to get in sync with each other. That's where you come in. How are the lessons going?"

"Pretty well. I'm getting less grief about them, and the men really seem to be trying. Now that they've settled down a bit, we can begin looking for some progress."

"It can't come a moment to soon," Brad grumbled as the visiting team began coming onto the field.

66

Even this early in the season, the Challengers held an undisputed lead in their league. Last year's Super Bowl winners, they were renowned as an implacable football machine, equally skilled at both offense and defense.

Brad downed his champagne and shook his head glumly. "It's more of our great luck that we play them twice this year."

"They look tough," Karla murmured, unable to tear her gaze from the giants milling around on the edge of the field. Logically she knew that the Flyers were every bit as large and strong, but just the thought that Mac would be going up against those moving mountains horrified her.

"They are," Brad confirmed, "and as mean as they come. The Challengers are famous for always walking a thin line on the rules. They'll take everything they can get, and they don't always care about fair play."

Karla wasn't sure what that meant, but she gathered it was nothing good. Tensely, she watched as the Flyers appeared. Even through the thick glass windows, she could hear the muted boos and catcalls of their so-called fans.

Mac and the men with him ignored them. They were there to do a job. The fickle crowd might not have existed for all the notice they gave it. But Karla couldn't help but wonder how she would have felt if an audience had reacted like that to her mere appearance on stage. It couldn't be very pleasant to start out with the spectators already expecting the worst.

For a while it seemed as though even the surliest fan was going to have to admit that the Flyers were in unusually good form. After winning the toss and electing to receive, Mac led the offense in a relentless march down the field, coming to within twenty yards of the Challengers' goalposts.

"You'll notice," Brad said at one point when there was a momentary lull in the action, "that he's not putting the ball in the air. Too damn many of his passes have either been incomplete or been intercepted this year. So he's going for slow, steady gains on the ground."

"Makes sense." By drawing on her own admittedly slim knowledge of the game and Brad's running commentary, she was able to understand most of what was happening on the field. In particular, she watched the wall of Flyers linemen, who stood between Mac and the opposing team, preventing the Challengers from getting at him while he set up each play.

The protection worked fine while the Flyers covered another fifteen yards and came within what Brad called "spittin' distance" of the goal. The crowd was on its feet, cheering now. Mac got the ball, fell back, prepared to hand off to the designated receiver . . .

A wall of human flesh drove through the linemen and hurled itself at him. Before he could release the ball, he went down hard, buried under a writhing mass of muscle and sinew.

Whistles blew, Brad cursed; the crowd screamed its contempt. Karla heard nothing of it. She could only stare white-faced at the field, her hands clenched and her body trembling.

When at last Mac was helped to his feet, she moaned softly. He walked off the field on his own, but from her point of view he might as well have been

68

carried off. He looked dazed and shaken, his face bleak. What had been a game seemed suddenly a grim, dangerous conflict.

"He won't come back, will he?" she asked shakily.

"What? Of course, he will. He wasn't hurt."

"But he could have been!"

Brad looked at her oddly as he said, "Honey, Mac knows how to fall and how to protect himself when he's down. It takes more than a single sack to stop him."

"You mean it could happen again?"

"The way things are going, it's bound to. His protection just isn't there."

By halftime, Karla knew what he meant. Mac had been sacked five times. No matter how quickly he tried to get the ball off, the Challengers were faster.

Again and again, he was buried under hundreds of pounds of angry, snarling opponents, until it seemed impossible that he could emerge undaunted. Yet somehow he did, though clearly at an ever increasing cost. As the buzzer finally sounded, the score stood at 7–0, with the Challengers winning.

"It could be worse," Brad insisted as he refilled her glass. "The boys on defense are holding the line pretty well." A humorless laugh escaped him. "Probably because they feel sorry for Mac and the beating he's taking."

"How much longer can he be expected to go on like that?" Karla demanded, making no effort to hide her outrage. "It's barbaric!"

"It's football, honey. That's the game. Mac's a pro. If we tried to take him out now, he'd have a fit." When she still glowered at him, he added gently, "How many times have you danced when you were hurting? How many times have you gone on stage with strained muscles and tendons? How many times have you finished a performance with your feet bleeding?"

Karla looked away. She knew he was right; in Mac's position she would undoubtedly insist on staying in the game. But knowing that didn't make it any easier to watch as halftime ended and the teams returned to the field.

Ten minutes into the third quarter the score stood at 13–7. The Challengers had scored another touchdown but missed the point after. The Flyers had retaliated with a fierce onslaught that at last got them on the scoreboard.

With his ground game blocked at every turn, Mac had finally been forced to put the ball into the air. He threw with incredible speed and accuracy, yet with the exception of that single score, every pass was incomplete. Often they missed by inches, because the designated receiver was a split second too slow or fast.

"It's a game of inches," Brad muttered. "That's one of the all-time clichés of football, but it's still the truth. Inches and seconds make the difference."

"I'm beginning to see what you mean by the lack of coordination," Karla said. "Individually, the players all look good. It's just when they try to work together as a team—"

"That's exactly what they aren't, and the best effort in the world won't change it. Only time and work will bring them together. I'm just hoping that you'll provide a little shortcut."

"And I'm just hoping they'll make it to my next

class. The shape they're in right now, I have to doubt it."

Brad cast a weary eye down the line of players slumped on the bench. As the fourth quarter began, every man looked exhausted and depressed. "They're starting to think of themselves as losers. That's a big part of the problem."

With seemingly superhuman effort, Mac managed to bring the ball into touchdown range yet again. With less than a minute left on the clock, he fell back for a final pass.

Karla held her breath, straining forward in her seat. Even the crowd was hushed. For the first time that season, the Flyers had a real chance at victory. If they could only hold the line . . .

They couldn't. Before Mac was able to release the ball, he was sacked yet again. Groans and derisive whistles reverberated through the stadium as time ran out. The jubilant Challengers trotted off the field congratulating themselves on their unbroken winning streak while the Flyers followed morosely.

Mac was among the last to leave. He had paused to speak with a dejected young player. Helmet in hand, his big body slightly slumped in fatigue, he seemed to be speaking gently and patiently. The boy looked relieved when they finally headed toward the ramp leading to the locker rooms.

Before they could reach it, one of the spectators took it upon himself to voice his anger over the loss in concrete terms. Hoisting what looked to be the last of a long string of beers, he threw the full can straight at Mac while shouting obscenities.

Karla jumped to her feet, all the color draining from her face as the missile struck Mac's shoulder.

He winced and turned toward the bleachers where security guards were already subduing the man. The stream of invective flowed over him, seemingly without impact. But she could see the stiffening of his body and the bleakness of his eyes as he walked away.

"Come on, honey," Brad said gently. "I'll have my driver take you home. I want to hang around and talk to the boys."

"I'll stay. I want to see Mac."

The distress in her eyes made him wince. Carefully he explained, "That's not a good idea. Take my word for it. After a game like this, Mac always wants to be alone. He won't even talk to me before tomorrow."

"Is that true . . . ?"

"Absolutely. He's been that way from the beginning. If you try to see him now, he'll be real uncomfortable, and he'll make you feel the same way." Quietly he added, "Mac's a very private person, Karla. Not unlike yourself."

That brought her up short and derailed her determination to go to him. Ever since their first meeting, she had sensed some point of accord between their seemingly divergent natures.

Perhaps Brad had just put his finger on it. They were both strong, self-directed people who needed to lick their wounds alone. Much as she longed to be with him, to offer whatever comfort she could, Karla felt she had no choice but to respect his privacy.

Reluctantly, she accepted the offer of a lift home. The trip in the limousine was swift and quiet, but she didn't notice.

She was too busy thinking about the way Mac had

looked down on the field, hurt and angered by both the loss and the savage reaction of the so-called fans. Hot tears blurred her eyes as she thought of how desperately he had fought. All too clearly she could imagine the pain he must be feeling, both physically and emotionally.

As she reached her apartment and walked slowly up the stairs, she regretted having left the stadium. No matter what Brad had said, Mac might have wanted to see her, if only to know that she was there and that she cared.

Seated in front of the fire, she tried hard to concentrate on her notes for the ballet she was choreographing, without success. The words and symbols might as well have been meaningless for all the impact they had on her.

Subconsciously, she was listening for some sound that, when it came at last, sent a shock wave through her. As the door bell pealed, she jumped up, her hands suddenly clammy and her breathing ragged.

"Who is it?"

"Mac. Can I come in?"

Her answer was to throw the door wide open, only to find him frowning at her. "You should have looked through the peephole first. What if I wasn't me?"

"You sounded like you," she pointed out reasonably even though she was feeling anything but. Telling herself not to read too much into his impromptu visit, she still could not keep her eyes from trailing over him.

The lean strength of his jean-clad legs and the power of his upper body clad in a plaid shirt and pullover could not conceal the weariness she sensed in him. Quietly she took the pizza box and six-pack of beer he carried into the small kitchen, as well as the bouquet of fresh roses.

She unwrapped the bouquet first, as he watched. "I remember you liked them. Are they okay?"

His uncertainty touched her as much as the gift. "They're beautiful." On impulse, she raised herself on tiptoe and brushed a kiss against his lean cheek. Before he could respond, she turned back to the counter and gestured at the other packages. "This is dinner, I presume?"

"If you don't mind. I did promise I'd bring some beer next time, and nothing goes better with that than pizza."

"Sounds good to me. I'll get some plates." Her matter-of-fact acceptance seemed to surprise him, but he said nothing more until they were settled in front of the fireplace, sharing the meal, the roses on the mantel in front of them.

"I heard you were at the game," he ventured at last.

Karla nodded noncommittally. "I went with Brad."

"Not quite what you expected, was it?"

She looked up, meeting his eyes. "It was horrible."

"Oh, come on, we didn't play that badly."

Brushing off his attempt at lightness, she said, "You know perfectly well that isn't what I mean. I've never seen anything so brutal in my life. And the crowd—it was like a Roman circus." Her eyes flashed as she made no effort to hide her contempt.

"When we win," Mac ventured cautiously, "they love us."

"Do you care? What good are they if they can turn on you like that?"

"Most of them don't. You're only aware of the others because they make the most noise."

"And throw things," she pointed out tartly.

He rubbed his shoulder gingerly. "That's pretty unusual. You shouldn't let one nut sway you against the entire game."

"I'm not. It was those nuts who were down on the field with you I'm worried about. Do you realize," she demanded quite seriously, "that what those men who kept sacking you did amounts to assault, and if they did it out on the street, they'd be arrested?"

Mac tried hard not to laugh. It hurt his bruised ribs too much. "It's the guys who were supposed to be protecting me who should be brought up on charges. But they feel badly enough as it is."

"As badly as you?"

"Yes, in their own way," he said quietly. "No one comes out of a game like that without feeling the effects."

"Mac, how much more of that can you take?"

"I don't know." Rather grimly he added, "But I've got an idea this may be my year to find out."

"You mean it could just go on like that all season?" The dismay she could not hide made him smile gently.

"Not if you succeed in teaching the troops a little style." Leaning forward, he touched her cheek gently. His breath was warm against her skin as he murmured, "I'm counting on you, darling."

Karla swallowed hard. Just then, she suspected she would have agreed to help him in any way possible. As he moved closer, her lips parted. She wanted so badly to kiss him. . . .

Mac winced. He sat up suddenly, his face taut. "Damn shoulder. I put some liniment on it before coming over here, but it doesn't seem to have helped."

Hiding her disappointment, Karla suggested, "Why don't I massage it for you?" At his startled look, she added, "Dancers are used to dealing with all sorts of aches and pains. I'll bet I can fix you right up."

"I'll bet you can, too," Mac muttered as he reluctantly allowed her to help him over to the bed. As he lay down on his stomach, he cocked an eyebrow at her. "You won't let this get out, will you? My reputation would be ruined."

"You're safe with me," Karla assured him lightly despite the tightening of her stomach and the wave of heat that spread through her. The touch of his lean, hard body beneath her was electrifying. Long moments passed before she remembered what she was supposed to be doing and moved her fingers gingerly. "Tell me if I'm hurting you."

"No . . . it feels great," he murmured sleepily into the pillows. "You beat Cootie any day."

"Who's Cootie?"

"The team masseur. Been with the Flyers for a couple of centuries. Great hands, but not like this . . ."

His appreciation helped make up her mind for her. If she was going to do the job, it'd be done right. Ignoring the rapid beating of her heart, she said, "Sit up and take off your shirt and sweater."

"W-what . . . ?"

"You heard me. I can't do much to help you if you keep all these clothes on."

Mac didn't argue further. Crossing his arms over his chest, he pulled off the sweater and tossed it onto the floor. Beginning to unbutton his shirt, he looked at her guardedly. "You're sure you won't try to take advantage of me?"

"Oh, you!" She took a swat at him, only to be playfully held off with one hand as he finished undoing the buttons with the other. When his shirt had joined the sweater, he lay back down on his stomach.

Karla took a deep breath, glad that he couldn't see her. The impact of his semi-nudity was startling. Accustomed though she was to supremely fit men, nothing had prepared her for the effect Mac had.

Her tongue darted out to moisten suddenly dry lips as she studied the burnished expanse of skin overlaying taut muscle and sinew. He had the look of a man who had known hard, physical work all his life.

Nothing else could account for the graceful symmetry of broad shoulders, powerful arms, and a sculpted torso tapering down to a narrow waist and hips. He was, she realized with a start, quite beautiful in a shatteringly virile way.

But that beauty was marred by the punishment he had taken during the game. A soft groan of protest rose in her throat as she took in the deep purple bruises and raw abrasions. Someone, a trainer perhaps, had tried to doctor them, with little success. They looked acutely painful and would undoubtedly remain so for some time to come.

Careful to avoid the injured spots, she began to gently massage the long line of his back where she

77

knew the muscles tended to be most tense after exertion. Mac sighed softly. His eyes closed. Beneath her skilled touch, his big body shifted slightly, becoming more relaxed.

"That's nice," he murmured huskily.

Karla smiled but said nothing. She was aware of what was bound to happen, but could not bring herself to interfere. Slowly, his breathing became deep and regular. The thick chestnut lashes shielding his eyes fluttered once, twice, then were still.

She kept up the soothing motion of her hands until she was certain he was fast asleep. Only then did she rise and go to the foot of the bed to slip off his shoes and draw the comforter over him.

An indulgent smile curved her mouth as she noticed that despite the size of her bed, Mac managed to take up most of it. He slept sprawled out, not unlike an exhausted child.

The humor of the situation struck her then. There were undoubtedly women all over the city, if not the country, who would have liked nothing better than to get Mac Gregor into their beds. She had managed it, only to have him fall promptly asleep.

Amusement tinged with tenderness kept her smiling as she went into the bathroom to wash her face and put on a nightgown. Returning to the bed, she gazed down at Mac, noting the strong lines of his face and the uncompromising strength of his body, visible even under the covers.

For just a moment, she hesitated. Then with a philosophical shrug, she climbed in beside him.

Karla frowned in her sleep. Something hard and

heavy weighed her down. Without waking, she moved, trying to shake it off.

She didn't succeed. Whatever held her pressed more firmly, as though to keep her in place. Her frown deepened. Not eager to leave the security of a sleep more relaxed and complete than any she had known recently, she reluctantly opened one eye.

Bright autumn sunlight streamed into the room, falling across the dark oak floor, the vivid quilt covering the bed, the long legs of the man beside her . . .

Both eyes opened, wide. She gasped softly and sat up, partially dislodging the sinewy arm lying just below her breasts. Mac murmured softly in his sleep but did not wake.

He was lying just as she had last seen him, sprawled on his stomach, facing her with his lips slightly parted and his lean cheeks dusted by thick lashes. It was hard to imagine how he could have looked more content.

He seemed completely oblivious of her presence, a fact she found perversely annoying. Memories from the previous evening flooded back at her, replacing her chagrin with a tender smile.

Against all expectation, he had come to her. Despite his need for privacy, he had sought her out.

Pleasure flowed through it, made all the more potent by the knowledge that it might not be lasting. When he woke, he might regret the impulse that had brought him to her.

But not if she had anything to say about it. Slipping carefully from beneath his arm, she went into the kitchen and put coffee on, but not before glancing at the mantel. The roses had fully opened. Their subtle fragrance perfumed the room.

Showering quickly, she brushed her hair until it fell glistening around her shoulders, sprayed on her favorite jasmine-scented perfume, and, without the flicker of an eyelash, popped herself into a violet silk robe that did little to conceal the beauty of the bare body beneath.

By the time she returned, Mac was awake and standing beside the bed with a wary look in his eyes. As their gazes met, she bit back a laugh. He looked as uncertain as a schoolboy. Moreover, he was blushing!

"Uh . . . good morning," he ventured cautiously.

A mischievous impulse seized her. Without pausing to think about the possible consequences, she smiled languorously. Brushing a tender kiss against his mouth, she purred throatily, "Good morning, darling. Isn't it a *lovely* day?"

Mac stared at her oddly before a quiet smile lit his eyes. Returning her kiss, he murmured, "Terrific, sweetheart. Absolutely terrific." Before she could reply, he captured her lips again, this time far more deeply and forcefully.

The firm, male mouth against her own made her tremble, as did the warm thrust of his tongue into her. Instinctively, she moved closer to him, savoring the exquisite sensations he provoked.

He was so big and powerful that in his arms she felt infinitely fragile. Yet the knowledge of how easily he could bend her to his will caused no fear. She knew, beyond the shadow of a doubt, that she had only to express the slightest objection to be instantly freed.

But escape was the last thing on her mind—she longed for more of the delicious contact with him. Through the thin silk of her robe, she could feel the hardening of his virile body. A soft purr sounded deep in her throat.

Mac's callused hands were warm and firm as he stroked her back. The long, lingering caresses sent tremors through her. When he at last raised his head and gazed down at her, she murmured, "You're not a bad masseur yourself."

He laughed gently, though his eyes were serious. "Thank you for letting me stay last night."

"You needed someone."

"No, not 'someone.' Just you." As surprised by that admission as she was, he let her go and ran a hand through his sleep-tousled hair. "Karla, I know we agreed to take it slowly . . ."

Bereft of his touch, she said the first words that came into her mind. "That was yesterday."

"And two days before that we hadn't even met. You know what's happening between us . . . what's going to happen if we keep on like this. I don't want you to have any regrets."

"You make it sound as though I'm the only one with anything to lose," she pointed out gently. "Are you sure that's true?"

"No," he acknowledged, bending to pick up his shirt. His movements were a bit stiff, but she could see most of his pain had gone. Putting his shirt on, he left it unbuttoned and followed her into the kitchen where she poured coffee for them both. Leaning against opposite sides of the counter, they regarded each other cautiously.

At length, Mac said quietly, "This is going to

sound like the worst line in the world, but the fact is I've never reacted to a woman the way I do to you. I want you so much I can hardly think of anything else, but I'm also scared of hurting you."

"I'm a grown woman, Mac. I can look after myself."

He didn't hide his skepticism. "You're also inexperienced in certain areas. You may not realize how risky a relationship can be."

"On the contrary. I know perfectly well that if I go to bed with you, I may end up getting hurt. But so may you. I've never believed decent, caring men can walk away from an affair unscathed. And that is what you are, whether you want to admit it or not."

He took a sip of coffee, regarding her over the rim of the mug. "So where does that leave us? Do we back out now or do we . . ."

Karla put down her cup. Very calmly, as though she had done it every day of her life, she put an arm around his waist and leaned her head on his shoulder. "When you were on the ten-yard line yesterday with only minutes to play and every chance of getting sacked again, did you back out?"

A low sigh of relief escaped him. With no further effort at reluctance, he placed the mug in the sink and wrapped both arms around her. Huskily he murmured, "No."

"Last month when I danced the lead in *The Firebird*, I hurt an ankle in the first scene. But I kept on and gave what may very well be the best performance of my career."

Looking up, she met his gaze with quiet certainty. "We're both risk takers, Mac, at least in our professional lives. The rewards have been great for each of us. Maybe it's time to take a few chances on a personal level."

A long, tanned finger touched her cheek gently. "You're sure?"

She waited through the space of a heartbeat before she nodded.

CHAPTER FIVE

"You're so delicate," Mac groaned moments later as he laid her carefully on the bed. "I'm almost afraid to touch you."

"Please don't be," she entreated, making no attempt at coyness. The heady confidence he instilled gave her the courage to be more honest than she would ever have thought possible. "I need you desperately," she murmured as her slender hands slipped past the opened flaps of his shirt to find the warm, smooth skin of his chest. "Don't deny me."

"Never, sweetheart," he promised thickly as he shrugged the shirt off and lay down beside her on the bed. His heavily muscled arms cradled her gently. His mouth was warm and seeking as he dropped feather-light kisses in the sensitive hollows behind her small ears, along the slender line of her jaw, coming at last to her yearning lips.

His tongue licked at the corner of her mouth, coaxing for entry. She gave it readily, as she would anything he desired. The playfully erotic duel they engaged in sent hot coils of fire spiraling through her.

Through the thin barrier of silk, her hardened nipples pressed against his chest. Her hands stroked the muscled width of his back, opening and closing convulsively as spasms of delight made her tremble.

When she felt his fingers on the hem of her robe, she lifted herself slightly to help him ease it off. The gleaming length of violet drifted unnoticed to the floor beside the bed as he gazed at her ardently.

Despite the unbridled intensity with which he scrutinized her, she felt no embarrassment. There was only pride in the knowledge that she could so enthrall him.

Hesitantly, as though fearful that she might vanish before his eyes, he reached out a hand to touch the creamy softness of her skin. "I've never seen anything as beautiful as you," he rasped.

Karla was almost beyond speech, but she managed to murmur, "You . . ." His head tilted quizzically, compelling her to draw a shaky breath before she tried to explain. "You're the one who's beautiful. I never knew a man could look like this. . . ." Her voice trailed off to a husky whisper as she gave into the irresistible urge to touch him.

The burnished skin beneath her hands was warm steel overlaid with velvet. Directly beneath the surface, she could feel hardened muscle and taut sinew. A thick mat of golden hair spanned the width of his upper torso before tapering down the concave line separating either side of his ribs to vanish below his belt.

Beneath her tentative exploration, his big body shook. Yet despite the driving intensity of his desire, he kept a firm check on himself as he began slowly, almost leisurely to love her.

A soft gasp escaped Karla as lean fingers stroked down her throat, along the graceful line of her shoulders, to find unerringly the sensitive skin of her inner elbows.

Mac lifted an eyebrow teasingly. "Ticklish?"

"A-a little."

"I'll have to remember that, if you ever get out of hand." Smiling down at her, his sherry eyes dark with need, he gently grasped her taut waist. As his work-roughened hands held her in their capable grip, the thumbs pressing into her sensually, he bent his head and nuzzled the high, full curve of her breasts.

His mouth was warm and slightly moist, his breath like satiny feathers against her heated skin. Dimly, in the back of her mind, she realized he was playing her like a finely tuned instrument perfectly accustomed to his touch. The capacity for resentment had deserted her. She could only glory in the knowledge of what he was doing to her and of what they would soon be sharing.

The slightest barrier between them was rapidly becoming intolerable. Karla's hands slid down his back, tugging unabashedly at the waistband of his jeans.

A low, pleased laugh rumbled against her. "Take it easy, sweetheart, I get the hint."

Moving away from her, he stood up beside the bed and began to unfasten his belt. She watched with frank delight and an enchantingly innocent curiosity that did not escape him.

Mac drew in his breath sharply. She was so damn lovely, and so vulnerable. He had never wanted a woman more or been more vividly aware of the need to go slowly and carefully.

He wasn't absolutely certain she was a virgin; that was a doubtful state these days in any grown woman. But there had been hints, indications, that if she wasn't completely inexperienced, she was very close to it.

The responsibility inherent in what he was about to do came close to overwhelming him. For a moment he wavered, torn between the need to protect her and desire beyond anything he had ever known.

Desire won, but only in a compromise. He could not resist the savage need to make her his, but he could take every possible care to make sure the experience was every bit as beautiful and fulfilling for her as he knew it would be for him.

Stepping out of his jeans, he hesitated only a moment before stripping off his jockey shorts, all the while watching Karla's reactions carefully. Her eyes widened and a flush stained her cheeks, but she made no attempt to look away. On the contrary, she seemed fascinated by him.

He was so . . . beautiful. There was that word again, but it was the only one that fit. The differences between them enchanted her.

As he returned to the bed, she met his eyes unflinchingly. What she saw in his gaze made her heart beat even more rapidly. He looked so . . . hungry, like a man starved of a fundamental necessity of life. Yet he was also uncertain, to a degree that made her yearn to reassure him.

Her slender arms raised to welcome him as her smile drew him back to her body. Groaning softly, he nestled against her. "Karla, don't let me hurt you."

Against his tangled hair, she crooned softly, "Don't worry about that. I'm not."

She was beyond fear, beyond doubt, lost to anything except the overwhelming sense of rightness that gripped her as he moved slowly over her body, gently preparing her for him.

As his tongue flicked over her aching nipples, his hand slid across the flat plane of her abdomen to the downy juncture of her thighs. There he paused, stroking her lightly until she arched against him in silent pleading.

A low growl sounded deep in his throat, an intensely male sound that found its answer in her soft moans. Drawing her breast into his mouth, he suckled her urgently even as he gave into the desire to learn her body fully.

Karla's hands fell to her sides, clenched with the force of the sensations tearing through her. The constraints of the world were falling away; she was free, soaring higher and higher to some shimmering peak of fulfillment she was just beginning to glimpse.

Mac drew back, prompting a sharp moan of protest. Despite the almost unbearable tension of his own passion, he managed to smile reassuringly. "Easy, love. Trust me. I want this to be perfect for you."

She tried to speak, to tell him he was already everything she could possibly want. But words were beyond her. Only the soft, helpless sounds of feminine arousal broke from her as he took her relentlessly to the very edge of completion before pausing again.

This time she didn't even try to protest. Instead, she simply reached for him with boldness that would not have been conceivable even a few minutes before.

Mac gasped as her soft, instinctively skillful hand closed around him. He shut his eyes briefly, struggling for control. When he opened them again, they were as dark as a storm-tossed sea.

"Karla . . . help me . . . bring me to you."

She hesitated barely an instant before the strangeness of what she was doing was vastly outweighed by the enticing sensations she could not resist. Mac murmured gentle words of encouragement and praise, and seemed to understand that for the moment she had gone as far as she possibly could.

Then he took over in a masterful display of virile skill and tenderness that left her gasping. Sliding his big hands beneath her buttocks, he lifted her tight against his body. The rough-silk hair of his chest teased her breasts even as his steely thighs engulfed her softness.

"Open your eyes," he ordered gruffly when she would have closed them. Obeying, she met his gaze and held it as he moved within her, at once confirming the full extent of her innocence and setting his seal on her.

It hurt, there was no doubt of that. Yet it was a strange sort of pain comparable only to what she had sometimes experienced at the most rapturous moments of the dance when her mind and spirit utterly overruled the protests of her body.

Mac had seen the sudden flash of pain that tightened her features and winced at it. "God, Karla, I'm sorry—"

"No, don't be . . . I want you . . . so much."

Her words and the ardent movements of her body beneath his banished the last of his doubts. Without losing his awareness of her vulnerability for even a moment, he began to move within her, patiently stoking the flames of desire until they threatened to consume them both utterly.

"Mac, please. I need . . ."

"I know, sweetheart," he muttered hoarsely. "I'll give you everything you need."

He kept that promise with shattering completeness. Despite the tremors that wracked his body and brought a sheen of sweat to his rough-hewn features, he held off his own ecstasy until hers was assured.

Only when he felt the sweet convulsions of her body rippling around him and heard her soft sobs of joy did he at last groan his pleasure into her mouth.

"I didn't know." Karla murmured long moments later as she snuggled against the hard wall of his chest. Lifting herself slightly, she gazed down at him in rapturous delight. "I'd heard about it, of course, but I really had no idea . . ."

Mac grinned teasingly. "I know." At her blush, his smile deepened and he laughed gently.

Resting her head against his shoulder, she asked quietly, "Do you mind?"

His big hand cradled the back of her head in a gesture that was at once comforting and possessive. "About your being a virgin? Hardly, but I have to admit I didn't fully expect it."

"I tried to drop a few clues," she reminded him gently. Her fingers tangled in the thick nest of curls covering his chest as she added, "I suppose in this day and age it must seem really strange to you that I hadn't—"

"No," he interrupted firmly, "it's just one more indication that you don't go in for halfway measures. And you're far too intelligent to have gotten entangled in casual relationships that would only have ended up hurting you."

"That's what I always told myself," she admitted, "but sometimes I did wonder if I just wasn't—"

"Wasn't what?"

"Very sexual." Before he could respond, she said hastily, "Oh, I know I can dance sensually, but that's different."

"I don't see how," Mac said gently, tipping her chin back so that she could not evade his tender gaze. "You are the sexiest woman I've ever known, and I can't believe you have any doubts about that now."

Karla laughed a bit shakily. She was stunned to discover that simply by lying so close to him, her legs entwined with his and the scent of his body filling her breath, the intense desires that had exploded within her only moments before were already stirring to life again. Huskily, she murmured, "I guess not. . . ."

He nodded very seriously. "Good." Sobriety evaporated as he could not resist the urge to add, "Because we've got a lot of lost time to make up for."

She wasn't about to object but instead had to stifle her disappointment when Mac abruptly recalled himself. "But not right away," he insisted stalwartly.

At her mutinous pout, he laughed tenderly and dropped a light kiss on the tip of her nose. "Believe me, sweetheart, there's nothing I'd like better than to make love to you again right now. But I promised to take care of you, and I mean to do just that."

Provoked by some ancient feminine impulse that

would not be controlled, Karla moved against him languidly. "Then we're in complete agreement."

Mac groaned deep in his throat. "I don't think so." There was a rueful gleam in his eyes as he tossed the covers aside and stood up. Standing over her, hands on his lean hips, he smiled indulgently at her fascinated scrutiny. "You should know better than to try to push your body too hard too fast."

"My body," she murmured distractedly, "does what it's told."

"And delightfully, too. But for the moment . . ." Too quickly for her to even think of objecting, he scooped her out of the bed and strode toward the bathroom. Setting her down gently beside the shower, he kept a powerful arm around her waist as he reached in to turn on the tap. When the water was properly warm, he stepped into the cubicle and drew her to him.

"Mac," she protested breathlessly, "I'm not in the mood for a shower." The sight of his magnificent body and the resonating echoes of the pleasure he could make her feel made it all but impossible for her to think coherently. But she was certain that there was only one place she wanted to be, back in the wide, welcoming bed lovingly entwined with him.

He chuckled gently. "I'll get you in the mood."

Karla gazed up at him, watching the rivulets of water running down his proud head and muscular neck to the massive width of his shoulders and chest. He looked like a burnished god standing before her, yet he was all the best that was human. A soft sigh escaped her as, once again, she gave herself up to his care.

Mac swallowed hard. The need to control his

desires was almost intolerable, despite the incredible pleasure he had experienced only a short time before. When he had only suspected her capacity for loving, it had been difficult enough to exercise restraint. Now that he knew it beyond the shadow of a doubt, his self-control was stretched to the limit.

In that small, private place where the scent of jasmine soap mingled with the musk of unbridled arousal, and the rush of water blocked out the sounds of the world, she called to him in the most eloquent way possible. Every movement of her body, every smile and look, was a siren song he could barely resist.

His need was impossible to hide. Karla gasped softly as he moved against her. Her light blue eyes opened wide. "Already?"

He chuckled wryly. "That's what you do to me, darling." Breathing raggedly, he added, "I think we'd better get on with this before I forget why I brought you in here."

"I never did think much of the idea," she pointed out pertly, not at all abashed by his rebuking look.

Holding her eyes, he reached for the soap and lathered his big, capable hands. "I'll have to change your opinion."

For long moments, she managed to stand still under his roaming touch as he knelt before her and gently but thoroughly began to wash her tapered legs. But as his hands moved closer to the seat of the desire he had so recently awakened, she shifted slightly, fighting the moan that threatened to break from her.

"Don't move," he ordered gruffly, raising his eyes for a single, compelling instant.

Shivering, she obeyed. As the sensitive skin of her inner thighs knew his touch, she trembled and found she could not stop. Not when he reached the rounded curve of her buttocks or the flat plane of her abdomen, and certainly not when he at last stood, huge and male, to caress her breasts with infinite tenderness.

By the time he was finished, she could barely stand. The riptide of passion he had fueled demanded satisfaction. Yet it was not yet to be. Handing her the soap, he muttered gruffly, "Your turn."

Karla bit the fullness of her lower lip, suddenly assailed by doubts. In the height of passion, she had known no hesitation about touching him. Instincts she hadn't realized she possessed had guided her unerringly. Or at least so it had seemed.

Perhaps she was fooling herself. Perhaps he had simply made allowances for her inexperience. What if he found her clumsy or inept?

Her doubts must have shown clearly on her face for he smiled tenderly. "Just do whatever feels right, sweetheart. Whatever you want."

What she wanted was to touch him, to explore the thrillingly male body before her, to delve into the mystery of how two such different beings managed to fit together so perfectly.

He gave her free rein to satisfy her curiosity until at last his restraint broke and he reached for her urgently. Burying his head in her sleek, wet hair, he muttered, "I hope you're recovered, love, because I honestly don't think I can wait any longer."

"Neither can I," she admitted candidly, and was rewarded by a devastating grin.

Lifting her from the shower, he dried her gently

despite the tremors coursing through him. But when she would have returned the favor, he stopped her and briskly did it himself. "No more, sweetheart," he rasped, "I'm not made of steel."

Engulfed in his massive arms, she tilted her head back to receive his devastatingly thorough kiss. Even as his hard, firm lips parted hers and his tongue probed her inner warmth, he was carrying her back to the bed.

This time their lovemaking was less gentle, but none the less fulfilling. Pierced by shimmering ecstasy, Karla cried out his name. She was dissolving, falling away from herself, being absorbed into the very essence of the man who moved so powerfully within and about her.

Mac was no less vulnerable to the forces their loving unleashed. All his barriers were falling, his heart and soul laid bare to the woman beneath him. The sensation was terrifying yet also welcome. It was right for him; the right time, the right woman.

All his life he had sought for her, in all the wrong places. Now she was his. As he brought them both to shattering completion, every thrusting move of his body was a silent vow that no one would ever take her from him. He would hold her close, against all the challenges of the world and their vastly different lives.

They spent all that day together, waking to make love again, then wandering outside to find something to eat. At a Japanese restaurant near Karla's apartment, they ate sushi served by a kimono-clad waitress while sitting on the floor of a private tatami room whose black lacquered table was decorated by a single lotus blossom.

Afterward, they strolled hand in hand through Central Park, savoring the vibrant colors of autumn and the shouts of children at play. Leaving the park reluctantly, they went to Mac's luxurious high-rise apartment so that he could pick up some clean clothes and shaving gear.

There was no question of where he would spend that night. They had no need to talk about it. Neither could bear the idea of being apart. Riding up in the elevator with him, Karla pressed herself close and murmured huskily in his ear, "You may be sorry for what you've done. I think I'm becoming insatiable."

"That's fine with me," he rasped, urging her against the burgeoning proof of his own desire. Playfully, he nipped her ear as he added, "You realize this is exactly what an athlete is supposed to avoid?"

Though his tone was teasing, she was instantly contrite. "Mac, I didn't think . . . If I'm lessening your chances to win . . ."

"On the contrary," he assured her quickly, kissing away her worried frown. "You're a positive inspiration, and when we get back to your place I intend to show you exactly what I mean."

Not entirely convinced, she murmured reluctantly, "Maybe we'd better not—"

"Don't even think that," he broke in, a lean finger caressing the delicate line of her throat. "You can't give a man a glimpse of paradise and then snatch it away."

The sincerity of his words warmed her, as much as the light of desire in his eyes. While she glanced around the apartment, he made short work of filling an overnight bag.

Zipping it up, he met her cautious gaze. "What do you think of the place?"

"Uh . . . you did say a decorator helped you with it?"

"I said a decorator *did* it. I refuse all responsibility."

Karla couldn't hide a thankful smile. The large, stiffly luxurious penthouse had nothing in common with the man she believed she was coming to know. Empty, she would have undoubtedly found it beautiful and a great temptation to furnish properly. But looking as though it had been lifted intact from a men's magazine, she found it hard and unwelcoming.

The angular leather furnishings, chrome lamps, and abstract paintings were undoubtedly expensive and fashionable. But they left her cold, while the man who lived among them did just the opposite.

Unable to stop herself, she blurted, "How do you stand this place?"

When she would have apologized, Mac stopped her with a gentle kiss. Opening the door, he said, "I don't. That's why I'm about to sell it to the Flyers' second-string quarterback, a rookie named Bill Easton." Glancing over his shoulder, he added cheerfully, "Bill loves this place. It's a ready-made stage set. All he has to do is add the girls."

"Is that what you did?" Karla asked softly as they got back in the elevator.

"Yes," he admitted quietly, making no attempt to mislead her. "I spent years playing that scene. At first it was great; I was doing everything I thought I should be doing. Trouble was it got boring fast.

Finally I woke up one morning and decided it wasn't worth it. I was feeling used up and empty inside."

"And now?"

"Now," he said softly, taking her arm as they left the building, "now I know what I was looking for all that time."

While the doorman summoned a cab for them, he added, "I got off that treadmill some time ago, Karla. Contrary to what the gossip columnists might make you think, there haven't been any women in my life in more than a year."

Helping her into the backseat, he added dryly, "And if you tell anyone that, my reputation will be shot to hell."

Before she could answer, the cabdriver interrupted. Hoisting himself around, he removed the cigar clamped between his jaws and nodded at Mac. "Hey, ain't you Gregor?" A bit warily, Mac nodded. "Hell of a game yesterday," the driver went on. "You must feel like . . . uh, excuse me, miss . . ."

"That's all right," she murmured lightly. Unbidden, the scene in the stadium flashed before her. Were they in for another diatribe from an irate fan? Casting Mac a worried glance, she saw the same thought had occurred to him. His features were taut, his eyes cold. He looked like a man ready for trouble and almost willing to welcome it.

Instead, the driver surprised them. Maneuvering the cab into traffic, he advised, "Don't let it get you down, Gregor. You're a damn good quarterback. Anyone with half a brain knows that. My money's on you every time."

"In that case," Mac said quietly, "you must have lost a bundle lately."

"So it hasn't been so great? So what? You aren't getting much help from the rest of the team, are you? Any chance they might get into shape?"

"We're working on it."

"That's what counts. Give it everything you've got and let the chips fall where they will. Am I right?"

Mac cast Karla a quick grin as he nodded. "That's all anyone can do."

"You bet. Let me tell you something. Driving this cab, I see things you wouldn't believe. People in this town are nuts. Why, they'll . . ."

With no further encouragement, the driver was off on a series of anecdotes about bizarre incidents he had encountered, which led inevitably into a description of the famous and near-famous he had shepherded at one time or another. He was just really getting going when they pulled up in front of Karla's building.

"Just one question," Mac asked the driver when he had helped Karla out and turned back to pay the fare. "What will you say when you tell people about driving us?"

The man laughed, accepting the generous tip. "I'll tell them you were with a real classy lady." Gunning the motor, he pulled away with one final bit of advice. "Your taste has sure gotten better, Gregor. Now just do as well on the field and you won't have a thing to worry about."

"What is it with taxi drivers in this town?" Karla asked bemusedly as they climbed the stairs to her apartment. "They've got an opinion about everything."

Mac shook his head ruefully. "It seems to go with

the job." As she unlocked the door, he added softly, "Anyway, he was right. You are a classy lady."

"You're not so bad yourself," she murmured, going into his arms without hesitation. Dimly, in the back of her mind, she knew the day was ending. Soon the world would intrude once again. Before that happened, she wanted to snatch all possible happiness.

Soon enough there would be time to think of the consequences of her actions. For the moment there was only Mac and the incredible pleasure they had found together.

She told herself it was enough. For the moment.

CHAPTER SIX

"I'm glad you decided to come along on this road trip, honey," Brad said. "You won't regret it."

Karla wasn't so sure about that. She felt ill-prepared to cope with the pressures of accompanying the team. After almost a week of Mac's very intensive company, the speed with which their relationship had developed was beginning to frighten her.

When they were together, she could think of nothing except the sheer, giddy delight of being wildly in love. When the demands of their careers forced them to be apart even briefly, she had difficulty concentrating and had to stifle her resentment over distractions which had once been the very purpose of her existence.

Unaccustomed as she was to needing anything except herself and dance, she was finding the barrage of new emotions and sensations unsettling, to say the least. The Flyers' road game gave her an opportunity

101

to put some distance between herself and the source of the turmoil raging within her, if only temporarily.

But she hadn't been able to take advantage of it. Faced with the choice of either making the trip or staying behind without Mac, she had chosen the lesser of two evils.

Or so she had thought. As she sat beside Brad for the short flight to Boston where the Flyers were to play the following day, she was beginning to wonder.

She and Mac had exchanged barely a word since he had left her apartment early that morning to pack for the trip. At the airport, he was all business, a quarterback and team captain concerned only with the well being of his teammates.

She had at least hoped they could sit together, but Mac apparently preferred the company of the other players. He was seated several rows back chatting with a couple of his pass receivers.

Karla stifled a sigh. She supposed it was for the best. If he had advertised their new relationship, she would have been very upset. Unfortunately, being all but ignored by him wasn't making her feel much better.

The sudden change in his behavior unsettled her and gave rise to all sorts of uneasy thoughts. Perhaps he was already regretting what had happened between them.

That didn't really seem possible, given the happiness they had found together, but she couldn't help but wonder. He seemed so distant and cold, so preoccupied by concerns in which she had no part. She shifted uneasily.

"Something wrong?" Brad asked quietly, putting a hand over hers.

"What? Oh, no, I was just thinking . . ."

"You don't mind flying, do you?"

Despite her gloom, she couldn't help but laugh. "I'd better not. I do it often enough."

"That's what I thought." He studied her for a moment. "I know I sort of twisted your arm to get you to make this trip. I hope you're not worrying about the work you left behind."

"You didn't twist my arm," she corrected him gently. "If I hadn't wanted to come along, I wouldn't have."

He nodded approvingly. Brad was one man who genuinely appreciated self-assertiveness in everyone, including lovely young women. "You're going to enjoy this, you know. It'll give you a whole new slant on the team and how it works together."

Taking the opportunity to shift attention from herself, she said, "I may be jumping the gun a bit, but it seems to me that the workouts are beginning to have an effect."

Since the previous weekend's loss, she had drilled the team daily. There was still some resentment, but results were beginning to show. Down on the field, where it counted the most, Karla thought she could see improved synchronism of movement, a greater tendency to move in rhythm with each other.

But it remained to be seen if that could be translated into a winning game. The next day's confrontation would give a good indication.

"I suppose everyone's tense about the game," she ventured.

"More even than you may realize. If we don't win tomorrow, the Flyers will have absolutely no chance of a championship. Even with a win, it will be very difficult, but at least the possibility will remain. Without it, the players will have a hard time making it through the rest of the season."

"Is the Boston team tough?"

Brad laughed humorlessly. "They aren't called the Victors for nothing. They've won the Super Bowl three times. After their defeat in the playoffs last year, they're out for blood. So far this season they haven't lost a game." He slumped slightly in his seat, reaching for the cup of coffee on the tray in front of him. "I'm afraid they think we're easy pickings. A walk-over."

"Then they're in for a nasty surprise," Karla insisted firmly. "The Flyers have just had a run of bad luck. We're due for a break."

Casting her a perceptive glance, Brad laughed gently. "When I asked you to help out with the guys, I knew you'd do a good job, but I didn't expect you to get very involved. I was wrong though, wasn't I? You've really signed on."

She looked away hastily, but not before he caught her faint blush. "I just resent the idea that the Flyers are a losing team," she murmured. "The men are all fantastic athletes and they work very hard."

"Too bad that's not enough to win games," he pointed out morosely.

"They'll win. You'll see."

She caught sight of Mac, still deep in conversation with the other players, as they got off the plane in Boston. He joined them on the bus to the hotel, leaving her to go with Brad in the limousine.

"How about dinner tonight?" Brad asked while they waited for their room keys. "The team's on curfew, of course, but that doesn't apply to you and me."

Karla doubted she would be very good company, but she agreed nonetheless. "Just give me half an hour to change, all right?"

"Fine. I want to have a word with the coaches, anyway." He grinned unrepentantly. "They're never too happy when I go on the road with the team, but it's hard to tell the owner to stay home."

Under the circumstances, she could well understand why he had wanted to come along. Though he tried to make light of it, she knew his constructive interest meant a great deal to the team.

Unlike many other owners, Brad never interfered in areas outside his expertise. Nor did he single out anyone for blame. In a quiet, understated way he provided solid support and commitment that meant every bit as much as the money he put up to get the best possible players and coaches.

He deserved to win, Karla thought as she slipped out of the jeans and sweater she had worn for the flight and replaced them with elegantly tailored wool slacks and a silk shirt that she wore under a velvet blazer.

Her room was large and comfortably furnished, but she couldn't help but note that it was several floors away from where the team was billeted. A gleam of amusement, the first in many hours, shone in her eyes as she wondered whom that was supposed to protect, her or the team.

Brad selected a seafood restaurant near the harbor for dinner. Over broiled lobster and cold beer, they deliberately avoided talking about the team. She didn't have to be warned that even the most seeming-

105

ly innocent comment dropped in public could make its way to the opposition with unforeseen effect.

By the time they had refused dessert and returned to the hotel, she was feeling more relaxed and less down in the dumps. But that mood didn't last long.

Once Brad had left her at her door with a fatherly peck on the cheek and the admonition to get a good night's rest, she found herself wide awake and fidgety. She missed Mac terribly. After the enthralling nights in his arms, being alone was frustrating and disquieting.

Lying in bed, staring up at the ceiling, she wondered what he was doing. On the road, he generally shared a room with Bill Easton, the new young quarterback who was his likely successor. They would have had dinner with the rest of the team and retired early.

On the eve of a game, the rules said they couldn't drink, stay out late, or engage in what was euphemistically referred to as "stressful activity deleterious to game performance." That translated to no sex.

All very well for him, she groused as she turned over yet again seeking a comfortable position. None was to be found. Vivid memories of their lovemaking returned to mock her.

Was Mac having any better luck getting to sleep? Probably. After all, he was used to being on the road, used to putting everything out of his mind except the game. If he was wakeful, it was undoubtedly because he was worrying about the outcome of such a crucial match.

That thought annoyed her. It didn't seem fair that she should be tormented by her need for him while he could close himself off completely and concentrate on other things.

Though she couldn't claim any great experience in such matters, it seemed to her that his behavior that day had hardly been that of a man in love. Not when he could acknowledge her presence with no more than a cool nod and essentially ignore her.

But then he had never said he was in love, had he?

Twisting in the covers, she groaned softly. The tender words he had murmured to her in the heat of passion hardly counted as a declaration of intent. They were simply one more aspect of his skill as a lover, his ability to put her completely at ease and make her yield to him unrestrainedly. The source of that skill ate at her.

He was accustomed to beautiful, sensual women who understood the game of "love" as well as he did. They had been part of his life for years. Now he said he was tired of all that and wanted something more. But did he really?

Sitting up, Karla plumped up the pillows and frowned at herself. It wasn't like her to be so insecure and apprehensive. What had happened to the inner calm and assurance she had always been able to count on?

It seemed to be gone as thoroughly as her unlamented virginity but with far more drastic consequences. Her body she had joyfully surrendered to Mac; her mind and spirit were another matter entirely.

She was far too intelligent and strong-willed not to resent the ease with which he had come to dominate her thoughts. Her every emotion seemed to suddenly depend on him. The core of her identity, her view of the world, even her moment-to-moment mood, all had shifted away from her and toward him.

Under other circumstances, she might not have minded so much. But they were so very different in outlook and experience. How could she allow him— or trust him—to look after her?

Yet how could she not? The decision was already made, the die cast. She had gone too far, too fast, to turn back now. He had her—heart, soul, and body. Whether he understood the package deal he had gotten and, most importantly, whether or not he wanted it remained to be seen.

Lying awake worrying wouldn't change anything. Or so she tried to tell herself. The first gray light of dawn was beginning to break over the horizon before she finally drifted into an uneasy sleep that ended all too soon.

Bleary-eyed and depressed, she went through the motions of showering and dressing before facing the new day without enthusiasm. Boston was not at its best. Rain threatened, and the wind from the northwest was cold and damp.

Perfect football weather, she supposed. Also perfect for her mood. Chomping morosely on a slice of toast, she tried hard not to think of the breakfast she and Mac had shared only the morning before.

That enchanted interlude might have been part of someone else's life and memory. She could hardly imagine herself as the languorously fulfilled, dizzyingly happy woman to whom the future had appeared infinitely promising.

She really had to get a better grip on herself. This endless fretting wouldn't change anything. Besides, she had a class to teach that morning. The knowledge that she would soon see Mac brightened her outlook, but only temporarily.

Barely had she arrived at the training area set aside for visiting teams beneath the Victors' stadium when she regretted getting out of bed at all. The players were in a foul mood, nervous and testy.

They showed no inclination to go along with her as she tried putting them through a few simple exercises intended to help them loosen up. Instead, they reverted to their behavior of the first day, opposing her at every turn. Worse yet, Mac acted no differently from the rest.

"We don't have time for this today, Karla," he growled finally, just when she had about decided it wasn't worth the effort to persist. "Not with the game coming at us."

As she stared at him in hurt surprise, the other men nodded their agreement. "I've had it," Mike Wolanski muttered. "Harris may think he can make us jump through rings just 'cause he's the owner, but he's wrong."

"You said a couple of days ago that this wasn't so bad after all," she reminded him quietly, with far greater forbearance than she was actually feeling.

"That was different. It's not the same when we're going into a tough game."

"I know that. But the workout will help you relax. You don't want to go on the field with any unnecessary tension."

"Honey, there's only one thing you can do to help ease my tension," he drawled insolently, his eyes raking over her, "and putting us through these fancy moves ain't it."

"That's enough, Mike." Stepping forward, Mac

switched off the tape machine that had provided a low background of music for the exercise. He yanked a towel from a nearby bench with unnecessary force and began to wipe the sweat from his face. "She's just trying to do her job."

"Since when are you in charge of protecting Little Miss Muffet here?" the linebacker demanded. "I don't see no personal property stamp on her."

Karla opened her mouth to protest, vehemently, the mere idea of that, but Mac forestalled her with an arrogant flick of his hand. His eyes were cold as he met the other man's gaze unflinchingly. "Look again."

The words fell into the sudden silence with deafening force. The men glanced warily from her to Mac and back again. Their scrutiny seared Karla.

She deeply resented having her personal life so abruptly exposed. She was angered by Mac's presumption that she could not handle the situation herself. And, after the difficult night she had endured, she was dismayed by the ripple of pleasure that had moved through her when he announced his possession.

Violent, contrary emotions clashed within her, causing an uncharacteristically impulsive reaction. "If you want to look at something," she snarled, "make it yourselves. Your attitude stinks. You act like a bunch of scared little boys afraid to face up to reality."

Fighting the sudden sheen of angry tears that turned her eyes to luminescent pools, she faced them squarely. Her voice trembled only slightly as she said, "At the beginning of the season you had an excuse for losing. You hadn't been together long

110

enough as a team. But that doesn't wash anymore. If you lose today, you'll have only yourselves to blame."

Striding over to the table where she had left her bag, she snatched it up and headed for the door. "I've had it. You won't cooperate, won't even try. If you were dancers, you'd never make it out of the chorus. Brad has a lot of faith in you. I'm sorry it's misplaced."

Even Wolanski looked abashed as she stormed out, but Karla didn't notice. She was too overwhelmed by anger and hurt. All the doubts and insecurities that had begun to plague her the day before were back in force.

She could think of nothing but the coldness in Mac's eyes and how reluctant he had been to even look at her. What a fool she had been to think they could make a life together when there was so much to keep them apart.

Engulfed in misery and all but blinded by tears, she was not prepared for the hard hand that suddenly grasped her arm. She was spun around and hauled up against a rock-hard chest before she could even begin to object.

"I think," Mac growled ominously, "that we'd better have a little clearing of the air in here."

At the sight of her tears, his expression softened. But Karla failed to notice. Startled by his sudden appearance, she jerked her head back toward the exercise room. "I thought that was what just went on in there. You stamping your brand on me and all that. A bit hypocritical, wouldn't you say, since you haven't been bothered to speak to me since yesterday."

For a moment he did no more than stare down at her bemusedly. Her angry sarcasm took him aback. But he rallied quickly and promptly enraged her by throwing back his head and laughing.

"Is *that* what this is all about? A little healthy female temperament? Thank God! For a minute there I thought you were really angry."

"I am! If you think you can ignore me, pretend I don't even exist, and then suddenly turn around and announce to the world that—"

"Not the world," he interrupted mildly. "Just twenty-one guys and a couple of coaches."

"You know perfectly well what I mean! You had no right to—"

"To say that you're mine?" His voice dropped an octave, becoming velvet sheathed in steel. "But you are, Karla. There isn't any doubt of that."

If she had been more in control of herself and feeling less vulnerable, she would have heeded the note of warning in his voice. But as it was, she chose to ignore it. Very clearly, she said, "I don't belong to you, Mac. People can't own each other. But even if that were possible, it wouldn't apply in our case. We're just too different."

"Is that so?" he inquired with deceptive mildness, his callused fingers stroking up and down her slender arms protected only by the thin sleeves of her leotard.

"Yes," she murmured tightly, struggling to ignore the sensations he so effortlessly unleashed. "We rushed into something because of a certain physical attraction. But that doesn't mean—"

"That doesn't mean I'm going to let you back out just because you're a little scared and upset."

Karla opened her mouth to retort, only to find there were no words. She could only stare at him mutely as she tried to assimilate the full extent of the vast gulf between them.

It seemed unbelievable that the man who had held her so tenderly such a short time before and raised her body to such exquisite heights of ecstasy could be so arrogantly oblivious.

Did he really think she wouldn't react to his behavior of the day before, that she would just quietly accept whatever he chose to dish out? Was she supposed to simply endure his abrupt change from complete disregard to macho swagger?

She was a full-grown woman, damn it! A thinking, feeling person every bit as intelligent and determined as he was. She wasn't about to let anyone treat her like this. Maybe her life before Mac had been lacking in something, but at least she hadn't been so horribly vulnerable and confused.

Angry at him, at herself, at the vagaries of fate that decreed she could care for a man she had so little in common with, she lashed out. "Let me go, Mac! I don't have to put up with this kind of treatment from you or anyone. If you think you can pretend I don't exist just a few hours after you've crawled out of my bed, you've got another thing coming. I've got too much respect for myself to put up with that kind of crap!"

His hands tightened on her arms as his face darkened. "Karla, you've got it all wrong. I had to try to put you out of my mind before the game. You don't realize the effect you have on me. If I let myself think about you, I wouldn't be good for anything else."

Regretfully, he shook his head. "I never meant for you to be hurt."

"Then you blew it," she snapped, not at all mollified by an explanation which at that moment sounded too pat to be true.

The sudden bleak look in his eyes surprised her. She watched, warily, as he said, "I refuse to believe that. This is all a misunderstanding. I hurt you, and now you're doing the same to me."

He was about to continue when a sudden shout from farther down the corridor drew his attention. One of the coaches was standing there, tapping a foot agitatedly. "Come on, Gregor. You've got to get suited up."

"In a minute. I—"

"*Now*, Gregor. It's twenty minutes to game time."

"Damn it! I don't need this right now. Karla, please listen to me. I'm sorry, I wasn't thinking . . . this caring about someone else is so new to me. Give me a chance to get used to it. Give us both a chance."

More moved by his heartfelt plea than she cared to admit, she was tempted to give in to him completely. But the hurt was still too fresh and her doubts still too great. Equivocating, she murmured, "Go play your game, Mac. That's what's important to you."

She hadn't meant that anywhere near as harshly as it sounded. All she had intended was a simple acknowledgment that at that time and place, the game came first. But Mac didn't take it that way.

A great stillness came over him. Shutters seemed to drop over his eyes, making him as remote and untouchable as a stranger. Even the bleakness she

114

had briefly seen vanished behind a self-protective mask.

"Mac . . ." she began tentatively, needing to reach him, to undo the damage she had—inadvertently?—inflicted.

He let go of her and raised a hand, cutting off her attempt. "Never mind, Karla. I get the message. You're scared of what's happened between us. I've punctured your neat little world and you're terrified of the consequences. All right, I can understand that."

His mouth twisted unpleasantly, testifying to the bad taste of that comprehension. "I may even decide it's worth the effort to set you straight. But right now, as you have so kindly pointed out, I have a game to play."

Her stomach tightened with regret as he turned away, the set of his shoulders implacable, and exasperation evident in every step. Longing to call him back, she did not. It was too late for that. The game wouldn't wait.

The angry words she had hurled at him echoed through her mind again and again as she changed her clothes and reluctantly went to join Brad in his box. She feared she was about to witness another Flyers loss, made all the worse by the fact that she might well have contributed to it.

Certainly she hadn't done Mac any favors by sending him off in such a dismal mood. Or so she thought. As the game began, she was forced to rapidly reconsider.

From the opening kickoff, the Flyers were clearly on the attack. They ranged over the field with stunning mastery, taking control of almost every play.

To the outrage of both the crowd and the Victors themselves, Mac called successful play after play. Five minutes into the first quarter, he had led his team to what turned out to be the first of many Flyers touchdowns.

"Way to go!" Brad shouted, on his feet, cheering wildly. Heedless of the supposed dignity of his age and position, he grinned broadly. "Those are my boys out there! Winners, everyone of 'em!"

So it appeared. Before the first half was completed, Mac had scored twice more while the Victors were held to a single field goal. The scoreboard read 21–3 as the teams left the field for a brief respite before resuming what looked to be a very one-sided combat.

The odds evened up slightly in the second half as the Victors came back with a touchdown, but Mac replied with a vengeance, throwing two more scoring passes. As one of his receivers executed a more than passable *jeté*, Karla could no longer contain her delight. All her fears and doubts were at least temporarily banished as she joined Brad's cheer.

The crowd howled its disbelief as the final seconds ticked away, and the scoreboard flashed the crushing results: 35–10, Flyers.

This time it was the opposing team that limped off the field, prompting a twinge of sympathy from Karla. But it was on Mac that her thoughts concentrated.

In the brief glimpse she had of him before he disappeared down the ramp to the dressing room, she saw not the elation she expected, but a firm, quiet determination that sent a shiver of apprehension along her spine. He had the look of a man who had completed one tough job and was now warmed up to tackle another even more difficult.

"Come on, honey," Brad urged, "let's go congratulate the guys."

She shook her head warily. "You go ahead. I wouldn't feel comfortable in the locker room."

He laughed teasingly. "Women sportswriters go in there."

"That's fine for them," she said firmly, "but count me out. You can relay my congratulations."

Brad tried once more to convince her, then gave in gracefully. He saw her safely to the waiting limousine that would return her to the hotel before he hurried off to celebrate with his team.

Half an hour later, she was seated in her hotel room, wondering what Mac was doing and wishing she was with him when someone banged on her door. Reluctantly she went to open it.

Barely had she unfastened the bolt when the door was pushed open and the object of her thoughts strode into the room. Standing tall and proud in expertly tailored mahogany wool slacks, a forest green shirt that matched his eyes, and a camel suede jacket, he dominated the small space as easily as he had the field.

She had only a moment to note that he looked fiercely determined and completely out of patience before he reached for her. "We've got a score to settle," he growled, hauling her against his rock-hard chest.

CHAPTER SEVEN

Weeks later, Karla still looked back on that scene in her hotel room with mingled bemusement and bewilderment.

The shock she had felt when Mac strode through the door was equaled only by her surprise when he abruptly let her go, slumped down in a chair, and regarded her narrowly.

"You're driving me nuts," he muttered. "I came here determined to be calm and collected, but I take one look at you and that goes out the window."

Hoping to conceal the sudden trembling that had seized her, Karla took a moment to lock the door and tighten the sash of her robe before meeting his eyes. Quietly she said, "Congratulations on the win."

He brushed that aside. "Thanks. Now let's get on to what's really important."

Her eyes widened slightly. "You don't think that is?"

"Only up to a point. Sure I want to win. For

myself and the team. But not as much as I've obviously made you think."

Too agitated to remain still for long, he hoisted himself out of the chair and began pacing back and forth. Before he arrived, the room had seemed spacious. But with Mac there, it appeared to have shrunk. Karla swallowed hastily. She could almost feel the walls closing in on her.

Trembling, she perched on the edge of the bed and stared at him. He looked tired and worried and . . . beautiful. She breathed in raggedly, her small tongue darting out to moisten lips that were suddenly dry.

So softly that he had to lean forward to hear her, she murmured, "Mac, why did you ignore me? You must have known how that would make me feel."

"No," he said shakily. "I didn't know, or at least I wouldn't let myself be sure. Part of me wanted to think you wouldn't care."

She shook her head dazedly. Why would he want her not to care? "I don't understand."

He ran a hand through his hair impatiently in a gesture she had already come to know. "I'm not used to women who care, Karla. My relationships, up to now, have been casual. The women I've known just wanted a good time, no commitments, no responsibilities. They were too caught up in their own lives to be able to cope with anything more."

"But you got tired of that," she reminded him gently.

"I sure did. I want more. The only problem is, now that I seem to be getting it, I'm not quite sure how to react."

His honesty took her aback even as she told herself it meant there was hope for them. As long as they could open up to each other, they had a chance. Slowly she said, "I'm not sure either, Mac. This is all so new that in some ways it's scary. I think maybe that's why I made such a fuss about being ignored. You see, I know what it's like to be so totally absorbed in work that nothing else matters. I didn't want to think you could do that to me."

"I can't. Every moment I spent away from you was hell."

The somber admission gave her the courage to go on. "You don't sound surprised."

He laughed harshly. "I'm not, but I can't pretend I'm pleased." Standing before her, he glared down almost reproachfully. "I've been in some tough spots but never anything like this." Gingerly, as though he thought he might be touching fire and didn't want to get burned, he brushed his fingers along her cheek before letting them curl gently around her small, firm chin.

This close to him she had no choice but to look up. He towered over her, at once infinitely large and male, yet at the same time unexpectedly vulnerable. The uncertainty she saw in his eyes made hers widen. "I'm no good at speeches," he said softly. "My strength has always been action, not words. It's hard for me to tell you how I feel when I don't understand it myself."

"Maybe you should start at the beginning," she suggested gently. "Why were you attracted to me in the first place?"

He dropped his hand but did not move away from her. "That's obvious. You're the most beautiful woman I've ever seen in my life."

"No, I'm not."

"What do you mean?"

"Just what I've said. There are plenty of women more beautiful than me." When he would have interrupted, she added quickly, "I'm not trying to be modest, Mac. I mean it. As a dancer, I have to know myself objectively, both the plusses and the minuses."

"You can say that and still claim you aren't beautiful?"

"Not in any classic sense," she assured him calmly. "My features are regular, my hair's pretty good, and my figure isn't bad." Smiling, she added, "If you want to believe I'm beautiful, that's fine with me. But I think there's another explanation for why you find me attractive. Besides, you've already admitted that you'd given up on beautiful women."

"They were different," he insisted defensively.

"In what way?"

"In *all* ways," he corrected. "Maybe you're right. I did see a lot more than just your looks from the first time we met." He grinned teasingly. "When you marched out of the exercise room and confronted us, I thought you were going to be eaten alive. I had visions of having to throw myself in front of your luscious body. Not," he added graciously, "that the sacrifice wouldn't have been worthwhile."

"Thanks," she murmured wryly, "but it's just as well it proved unnecessary." On a more sober note, she added, "Not that I have any illusions about how the guys think of me. Especially after today."

"You mean that dressing-down you gave us when we wouldn't cooperate with the workout?" He laughed wryly. "Honey, that's the best thing that

121

could have happened to the team. You made us confront what we were too scared to admit on our own. We went out on that field determined to prove we didn't really believe we were losers."

Karla laughed softly. "You certainly did that. I don't think the Victors will ever recover. They may have to change their name."

He shrugged dismissively. "Too bad for them." His eyes darkened as, more gently, he added, "Look, what I wanted to say . . . I meant it about not wanting to hurt you. If I'd been thinking about something besides myself, I would have realized how you'd react to being cut out like that."

"I was a bit taken aback," she admitted hesitantly.

"You were flaming mad, honey, and we both know it!"

"Well, maybe a little . . ."

"You had a right," Mac assured her. "The real problem is I can't guarantee it won't happen again." His gaze locked on hers as he said slowly, "Karla, I'm not used to revealing my emotions, not even to myself. I know I care about you a lot, more than any woman I've ever known. But that isn't what you want to hear, is it?"

She was silent for a long moment before she said very quietly, "Mac, I love you." At his startled look, she smiled almost apologetically. "You can't really be surprised. I think you know me well enough by now to understand that I would never have made love with you without really feeling love. It's only natural that I would want you to feel the same way about me, and to tell me that."

The light that had flared in his eyes at her quiet declaration gave way to confusion and concern.

122

"Karla, I can't lie to you. Maybe it just isn't in me to say those words and really mean them."

Careful not to let him see the full extent of her disappointment, she touched a gentle finger to his lips. "I don't want you to try to force yourself into a mold where you don't fit, Mac. I love you just the way you are. If you can't return that . . . I guess I'll just learn to live with it."

He gripped her wrist lightly, stroking the throbbing pulse point, as he murmured, "Why would you be willing to do that?"

"Because," she explained with almost brutal candor, "the alternative is even worse."

Mac winced but made no attempt to deny her words. Instead, he drew her closer, one hand on the slender curve of her hip as the other continued to gently chain her wrist. Thickly, he murmured, "Karla . . . I know you deserve better. But God help me, I can't refuse what you offer."

A low sign of relief escaped her. Pride might dictate that she hold out for an equal commitment, but pride was cold comfort when compared to all the warmth and joy he offered. One empty night without him had been enough to show her that.

With innate grace, she rose on her toes and brushed her lips lightly against his. "Then take me, Mac, and let the future take care of itself."

The blatantly sensual yet vulnerably innocent invitation was more than he could resist. A low growl sounded deep within his chest, and his hand tightened on her hip. Pressed against him, the rough fabric of his slacks rubbing against her thin silk robe, she was branded by the urgency of his manhood.

Karla responded without restraint. If she could

not have his heart, she would take what she could. Any lingering sense of timidity vanished as she slid her hands past the open lapels of his jacket and along the hard, taut line of the flesh beneath his shirt.

The tremor that promptly wracked him inspired her to go further. Flashing him a tender smile, she began to undo the buttons. The thick mat of hair covering his chest was warm and silky to her touch. She trailed her fingers through it slowly, surprised by the heat she felt emanating from his skin.

"Do you have any idea what you're doing to me?" he muttered hoarsely.

She raised an eyebrow innocently. "Undressing you?"

He laughed almost harshly. "I'm not sure how much longer I can stand this."

"I thought quarterbacks were trained for endurance."

"Lady, nothing—absolutely nothing—could have prepared me for you."

Pleased by that, she bent her head to reward him with light, teasing kisses along the massive width of his torso. Beneath her small, flicking tongue, his flat male nipples hardened. Drawing one into her mouth, she nipped it gently.

His callused hands closed on her shoulders. She was drawn irresistibly upward to meet his hungry lips. As his mouth claimed hers, his tongue fiercely thrusting inward, he slipped a leg behind hers and held her pinned to him in gentle bondage.

"Sweet, Karla . . . so sweet . . . let me . . ." With hands that shook, he undid the belt of her robe. It fell open to reveal the alabaster length of her body bared to his sight and touch. His heated gaze raked over her ardently, fueling the arousal that was already almost unbearably intense.

Small, sharp white teeth bit into her lower lip, prompting a husky groan from Mac. "Don't do that . . ." His tongue lashed out, soothing the slight marks she had left.

Karla's wide blue eyes were becoming glazed, and her breathing shallow. Far in the depths of her body she could feel the beating of great waves. Their power surged through her, carrying her farther and farther from shore.

Small yet strong hands reached for the buckle of Mac's belt. She undid it swiftly, with no attempt at coyness. It was important that he know how much she wanted him.

As her fingers brushed the hard flatness of his abdomen, he groaned. She had barely a chance to draw a breath before he lifted her high against his chest and carried her in rapid strides across the room to the bed.

After laying her down in the center with her midnight black hair streaming across the pillows, and the violet silk of her robe a startling contrast to the ivory purity of her body, he stepped away slightly. Without taking his eyes from her, he hastily stripped off his clothes before returning to her.

The touch of warm, taut maleness along every inch of her skin made Karla moan helplessly. Her head tossed back and forth against the curtain of her hair as her hands stroked the corded width of his shoulders, marveling at the immense strength beneath her seeking fingers.

He bore her touch through long, exquisite moments before the last of his self-control abruptly snapped. "Vixen," he groaned tightly. "She-devil. You look like an angel, but you—"

"*Yesss . . .?*" she drawled provocatively.

Ruefully, Mac laughed and nuzzled the satiny length of her throat. Turning over on his back, he drew her to him and he murmured, "You put the most accomplished courtesan to shame. Everything about you is perfect."

She wanted to believe him, but she couldn't help pointing out what he already knew. "I haven't had much experience. *Oh!*"

The sudden tightening of his teeth around her nipple put an abrupt end to her diffidence. Grinning roguishly, he said, "All the experience in the world can't hold a candle to genuine feeling." Mac frowned slightly as he heard his own words. He meant what he said but was nonetheless surprised by the truth of it.

Of all the women he had known, and there were a considerable number, though not anywhere near as many as the gossip columnists claimed, not one had ever moved him as Karla did. He had always enjoyed sex but thought of it as strictly recreational, a needed release from the pressures of the world and a particularly thoughtful accommodation of nature.

It was a shock to discover that he was capable of feeling far more. When he made love with Karla, he lost all sense of himself. Mac Gregor, football star, ceased to exist. There was only a man claiming, and being claimed by, his woman.

He felt overwhelmingly possessive about her for reasons that seemed to go far beyond the fact that he was the first lover she had ever known. When Wolanski had made that comment about how she could ease his tension, he had come damn close to smashing the linebacker's face in. And Mike was his friend, a man he had worked beside for almost ten years. Yet that hadn't meant a damn thing against his feelings for Karla.

When he looked at her he saw . . . what? Beauty and passion, certainly. But also intelligence, strength, courage. A woman who was a whole and complete individual capable of accepting and even glorying in the challenges of life. He wanted her to need him but not to be dependent on him. The distinction was a fine one, as he realized, yet he had no doubt that it was valid.

She filled him with joy to the very center of his being. But she also scared the living daylights out of him.

Even that silent admission made him flinch inside. His professional life was built around courage—the drive to prove himself again and again, to deny the physical limitations of pain and weakness. He didn't question why he was that way, he just was. It had served him well enough, until now.

Now he was up against something he couldn't resist . . . or understand. He had been drawn to her from the first, like a moth to a flame. He grinned wryly. He'd never make a good writer; he even thought in clichés. But that didn't lessen the truth of his comparison.

A cool, gentle hand touched his brow. "Mac, what's wrong?" Karla had sensed the emotional conflict within him and was distressed by it. He seemed so far away suddenly, and so worried.

"What . . .? Oh, nothing. Sorry, I just got distracted."

Her mouth twisted wryly. "That's not exactly flattering." The dull flush that stained his prominent cheeks made her stifle a laugh. "I'll have to see what I can do about holding your attention."

Before he could respond, she moved above him, just enough to provoke a sharp gasp. "Karla," he murmured thickly, "you have no problem at all holding my attention."

Her hands trailed down him alluringly. "You'll have to convince me."

"How . . . ?" The half-wary, half-entranced note she heard in his voice sent a shiver of delight through her. He was surprised by her sudden boldness but not displeased. Her sensuality was no threat to him.

Which was just as well, since she intended to give full rein to it. How amazing it was that so powerful and indomitable a man could tremble at her slightest touch. She had only to trail a hand across the sculpted muscles of his torso . . . to bend her leg slightly so that the silken smoothness of her inner thigh rubbed against his hardness . . . to press her lips gently to the corded column of his throat and taste with her tongue the faintly salty elixir of his skin . . .

A heady sense of power surged through her, similar to, but deliciously different from, what she experienced at the height of a dance. When he would have moved, she pushed him back gently against the mattress. With fluid grace she drifted over him, pausing to taste and caress and torment until at last he could bear nothing more.

The purely male growl that broke from him might have been menacing had she not so thoroughly shared his desire. Big, callused hands grasped her hips as he lifted her, holding her above him for a moment as their eyes met.

Gazes locked, he lowered her inch by inch onto him until at last they were fully joined. The piercing sense of being truly and completely possessed made Karla moan helplessly. Her head fell back, the silken fall of her ebony hair tumbling to the curve of her buttocks. High, full breasts lifted proudly, the taut nipples beckoning his touch. Her hands grasped his shoulders, bracing herself as she tried to sway to the rhythmic beating of her heart.

When she found that she could not, her eyes opened wide, meeting his with mingled bewilderment and frustration. Mac held her immobile, not hurting her in the least but making it impossible for her to fulfill her most desperate need.

The gentleness that was so often a part of their coming together was suddenly gone from him, swamped by fierce determination and something that looked perilously close to anger. She did not mistake the source of his emotion. Perhaps because she shared his sense of astonishment and wariness about what was happening to them, she understood what drove him.

"Feel me inside of you, Karla," he demanded hoarsely. "Feel what I do to you."

She had no choice but to obey. Still holding her clasped tightly to him, he moved within her so powerfully that she gasped. The velvety walls of her body were giving way before him, yielding and reforming to meet his demands. She was completely open to him, vulnerable as she had never been before in her life.

The flames he sparked were already beginning to

rage into an inferno that would soon consume her. But she was determined not to be alone in that moment of conflagration and rebirth. Every primeval female instinct she possessed demanded that Mac be fully with her.

He continued to hold her so firmly that she could only respond to his movements, not initiate her own, until it occurred to her that she had other resources at her command. An infinitely feminine smile curved her lips as she deliberately varied the rhythm of their union with powerful inner forces of her own.

Mac groaned deeply. His eyes flew open, meeting hers. "So sweet . . . perfect for me . . ."

And for her. She doubted a man and a woman had ever fit together more naturally or completely. Perhaps he was right about not being able to confront his emotions. But the beauty with which he claimed her left no doubt that those emotions were as real and strong as her own. Never had she felt more cherished. His every touch and movement made her vividly aware of herself as a woman capable of extraordinary passion, and of him as a man who gloried in her strength and matched it with his own.

They were together through every instant of the climb to a shimmering peak of fulfillment, together at the moment of completion when the world fell away and they were alone in a realm of their own creation, and together in the slow, gentle return to earth locked in each other's arms.

In the aftermath of their shattering release, Mac nestled her close against him. The firm male lips that had been so demanding on her flesh only moments before were gentled as he murmured, "My beautiful Karla . . . my own . . ."

The words reached her through a haze of sleep. A wave of all-encompassing contentment washed over her. Surely the superficial differences of their lives were only inconsequential details that could not mask all that they had in common.

They were both strong, impassioned individuals who had long ago dedicated themselves to demanding paths and were now reaping the rewards. They had come together at a time when each was ready for something more, ready perhaps for the ultimate commitment two people could make.

Mac was understandably concerned about what was happening to him. It was outside all his experience. She was the one accustomed to dealing with the realm of emotion. It was up to her to show him the way with love and patience.

He certainly deserved no less. After all, hadn't he already had the courage to come to her twice, once when he first claimed her as his own, and again that very day after she had sent him away in anger?

All she had to do was see to it that he kept coming back until he realized he simply wanted to stay.

Or so she thought.

CHAPTER EIGHT

Over the next few weeks, Karla was slowly forced to admit that her confidence in her ability to bring Mac around might be misplaced. He continued to be a tender, giving lover and caring friend who filled her days with quiet happiness and her nights with explosive passion.

But there remained a line over which he seemed unable to go. He offered her desire, affection, respect; feelings many other women would envy. Yet without love, none of them were enough. Certainly not if they were to have a future together.

And that, she was beginning to realize, was the problem. For a woman who had never before had an affair, she seemed to know a great deal about it. Enough, at least, to be sure she needed more.

Perhaps if her relationship with Mac had caused problems with her work, she would have been less certain about what she wanted from him. But on the contrary, her career was going better than ever.

Her imagination seemed to have sprouted wings. She soared on a continuous flow of creativity. Her dancing was magnificent, encompassing the strength and agility of a young woman and the maturity of an experienced *artiste*. Her choreography seemed to have broken through some invisible barrier. The interest and acclaim she received pleased her, but not as much as the quiet certainty that she was at last coming into her own.

At least professionally. Personally was another matter altogether. Sighing, she got out of the car and glanced around the stadium parking lot. The banners that were raised whenever the Flyers were playing at home fluttered in the breeze.

Winter had descended on the city abruptly. No lingering Indian summer this year. Instead, remnants of the previous night's frost still lay on the ground, and the dark swirl of clouds obscuring the sun hinted at winter's storms to come.

She drew the collar of her persimmon-colored wool coat up around her and shivered slightly. Not that she minded the weather. It was a good excuse to cuddle in front of the fireplace in her apartment. Mac slept there every night the team was in town. His clothes shared space in her closets, his shaving gear had a permanent place in the bathroom cabinet, and a supply of his favorite beer was always on hand.

He still teased her about her lack of furniture and other accoutrements of success, but she knew he found her home a much-needed refuge from the rest of the world. Just the night before, he had confided to her that he had never been through a rougher season.

As quarterback and captain of the team, the pressure on him was enormous. He was a constant target of fans and reporters. Hardly a day passed without some item about him appearing in the sports news. His every move was analyzed from the perspective of hindsight.

The irony of it all was that the Flyers were winning. Since their game against the Victors, they had remained undefeated. Sportswriters nationwide were marveling at their comeback. From a disastrous early season they were now within striking distance of the league championship.

There were many theories as to what was responsible for their success, including Karla's own role in the turnaround. News of the team's ballet workouts had leaked. The first response was disbelief and ridicule. Mac bore the brunt of that as he calmly deflected comments that would have had other players in an uproar.

As win followed win, the derision died away, slowly replaced by grudging respect. There were even rumors that some of the other teams had hired ballet coaches, but if so, it did no good. The invincible Flyer machine rolled on toward what gave every hope of being a winning season.

But not, Karla reminded herself sternly as she waved to the guard and headed toward the exercise room, if they got overconfident. Steady, persistent effort had gotten them this far; it could carry them the rest of the way, too.

The routine of changing into her leotard and pinning up her hair was so ingrained that she went through the motions with her thoughts firmly elsewhere. The previous day she and Mac had driven out to Long Island and walked miles along the deserted beach holding hands and talking about nothing in particular.

Afterward they had found a small seafood restaurant still open despite the end of the tourist season and gorged themselves on oysters and lobster. Back at her place, in front of a blazing fire, they had made long, glorious love before at last falling into bed and sleeping as peacefully as two exhausted children.

It had been a wonderful day that, oddly enough, had left her feeling mildly depressed. Perhaps because when she woke up that morning Mac was gone, off to early practice with the team. A note stuck to the refrigerator door made her laugh and blush at the same time but did not still the faint stirrings of doubt that were beginning to haunt her.

She wasn't making any progress with him. Every time she tried to get past the invisible barrier between them, he drew back. Just enough to dampen her spirits.

Not that she was anywhere near giving up, she told herself firmly as she began a series of stretching exercises. Ballet dancers knew more about discipline and persistence than just about anyone, including quarterbacks. Besides, for every moment of discouragement he gave her there were hours of warm happiness and incandescent pleasure she would not have missed for all the world.

When she heard the door of the exercise room open she smiled but did not turn around. The hard hands that gripped her waist and the warm mouth that explored the nape of her neck were no surprise. Mac had taken to arriving early for her classes so that they could have a few minutes alone. She appreciated his desire to be with her, but she couldn't resist teasing him a little.

Still not looking at him, she murmured, "What have I told you about being discreet, Walter?"

"Walter! Who the hell is Walter?"

Glancing up, all wide-eyed and innocent, Karla managed an abashed giggle. "Oh, it's you. Sorry. I have such trouble keeping everyone straight." She waved a hand airily. "You know how it is to be in demand."

"I know how a certain smart-mouthed ballet dancer is going to feel when she tries to sit down," he warned ominously.

"Threats will get you nowhere."

He grinned down at her unrepentantly. "How about this?" he murmured, his hands sliding along her back to cup the taut curve of her buttocks and urge her against him. "Where will this get me?"

"Arrested." The deep voice from the vicinity of the door made them both jump. Mac dropped his hands but looked not at all repentant as he laughed good-naturedly.

"She's over age, Wolanski. I checked."

The linebacker grinned, as did the other men who had missed nothing of the scene. Karla groaned inwardly. Her relationship with Mac was being conducted under the knowing eyes of his teammates who seemed to approve wholeheartedly. Even Mike Wolanski had mellowed in his attitude, giving her no further trouble since the day Mac had so clearly stated his claim on her.

When she adopted her best *premiere danseuse* manner and said, "Let's get to work," no one objected. The session went smoothly. The men were all accustomed to the movements by now and no longer seemed self-conscious about working to music. Of course, she was careful to pick pieces with a decidedly masculine flavor. The final aerobic workout was done to the strains of Ravel's *Bolero*, certainly powerful and stirring enough for even the most macho.

At its end, she spoke with several of the players who were recovering from injuries, recommending exercises that might prove helpful. She knew they were all deeply concerned about being in shape for the rest of the season. With all their earlier losses, every game was do-or-die for them. Even a single defeat at this stage could destroy all their hopes for a championship.

"Will you hang around for a while?" Mac asked when the last of the other players had left and they were alone again.

Karla didn't question his desire for her to stay during the practice sessions. She simply accepted it and welcomed the opportunity to give him whatever support she could.

"Sure. I figure if I watch enough, I'll finally get to understand the game."

He frowned slightly. "I thought I'd explained all the rules to you the other night."

She touched a hand to his lean cheek, smiling reminiscently. "Hmmm . . . and do you remember what else we were doing at the time?"

To her delight, he flushed slightly. "Oh, yeah . . . come to think of it, I can see how you might not have been paying any attention."

"I guess you'll just have to try again."

The gleam in his eye assured her that that was precisely his intention. Dropping a light kiss on her mouth, he muttered, "I've got to get going. We're putting in a couple more hours of field practice today."

"I brought my choreography notes with me. I'll sit in Brad's box and work on them until you're done."

Mac grinned gratefully. "Thanks, honey." He turned to leave, only to pause and look back at her. "I'm beginning to think you're some kind of good luck charm. Whenever you're around, everything works."

Deeply pleased, as well as embarrassed, she laughed huskily. "Don't let the guys hear you say that. They'll think you're serious."

His smile faded. Somberly he said, "The whole team feels the same way, honey. Nobody thinks it's just a coincidence that we started winning again shortly after you came on board."

He was gone before she could reply, leaving her to shower and change as she considered what a complicated man he was, capable of great warmth and generosity of spirit, yet doubtful of his ability to love.

Brad's box was snugly-warm despite the brisk wind blowing outside. She settled into it with the ease of familiarity. Before the colder weather arrived, she had watched the practice sessions from the bleachers. But with the drop in temperature, she was grateful for the protection the box offered.

Down on the field, the players were taking the weather in stride. Mac had explained to her how the first games of the season were often the toughest because they were played in ninety-degree heat. Everyone preferred the cooler weather when the heavy protective gear they wore was a help rather than a hindrance.

But watching them, she couldn't help but wonder how much protection they could have even under the best circumstances. The Flyers were known as an all-out team that held nothing back. Every man among them took chances that could inevitably lead to injuries. In the crunch of bodies, the thud of muscle and sinew, the high leaps and go-for-broke throws, the possibility of disaster always lurked.

Karla held her breath as one of the young pass receivers raced down the field and leaped a good six feet in the air, twisting his body as he did so to catch the ball Mac had hurled with such remarkable force and accuracy. That time the play had worked, but if either man had been off by even a split second the results would have been different.

She had seen receivers misjudge the angle at which they jumped, and come down hurting. And she had seen quarterbacks injure their throwing arms or fall beneath the onslaught of the opposing team because of a moment's error in timing.

So far, Mac had been lucky. In his long career, he had suffered only two major injuries. One, a fractured collarbone, had laid him up for several weeks five years before. The other, a damaged tendon in his left knee, had proved more persistent. Despite the best efforts of orthopedic surgeons, trainers, and masseurs, he often came off the field hurting.

Being no stranger to pain herself, or to how quickly it could occur, Karla found herself watching with particular care as Mac set up a new play the Flyers were just trying out and began running the team through it. The first three tries went fine; on the fourth everything fell apart.

She had no idea what caused it. The sequence of

events was too quick. One moment Mac was fading back to throw the pass, the next he was writhing on the ground, reaching instinctively for his knee, his face twisted in agony.

There's nothing I can do. The coaches will take care of him. If I go down there now, I'll only be in the way.

The whole time she was telling herself all this, Karla was busy jamming her papers into her bag and pulling on her coat. Racing out of the box, she dashed down the stairs toward the locker rooms just as Mac was carried in on a stretcher.

Determined not to let him see her near-panic, she slowed her pace and pinned a smile on her lips before approaching him. With feigned casualness that cost her more than he would ever guess, she said, "Looks like you'll be quitting early today."

Mac grunted his assent, but his eyes told her he was glad she was there. "Damn knee," he muttered, his teeth gritted against the pain. "I don't even know what the hell happened to it."

"It just went out, Mac," one of the trainers murmured quietly. "You know there's always that risk." Gesturing to the other men, he said, "Let's get him inside."

Mac's gaze locked with Karla's, asking the question he didn't want to put into words. "I'll be here," she said softly. He nodded, some of the tension easing from him as he was carried through the door and disappeared from sight.

The wait was longer than she had expected. In the head coach's office, empty except for herself, she paced and sat, sat and paced, all the while wondering how badly off he really was.

Knee injuries were tricky. She knew dancers who

140

had suffered from them and understood how suddenly they could turn serious. Mac's pain had been acute; not even all the years of stalwart conditioning and endurance could mask it.

What if he didn't respond to treatment? If Mac didn't snap back into shape, he would be replaced as quarterback. And that, she was certain, would be worse than any injury. In her mind's eye, she saw him going down again, the stamp of pain on his proud features, the agonized tautness of his magnificent body.

How unfair if he should have it all torn away from him just when it was in his grasp. She couldn't bear the thought of that, not knowing as she did how much it mattered to him.

She glanced at the clock on the wall again. An hour had passed. The need to know what was happening drove her from the room. Out in the corridor, several players were milling around. Though they wouldn't say so, she guessed they were also concerned.

Mike Wolanski took it upon himself to soothe her. "Don't worry," he said. "Mac's pretty tough. For a quarterback."

Karla nodded, fighting to blink back her frightened tears. This was ridiculous. She had been hurt herself, plenty of times. She knew it was a risk any performer took. Mac would be fine. He'd be back on his feet in no time, laughing as though nothing at all had happened.

When he walked through the locker room door doing exactly that, her mouth dropped open. He might have been a completely different man from the one who had been carried in there writhing in pain what now seemed a short time before. Elegantly dressed in tapered wool slacks, a silk knit shirt, and a suede jacket, he strode into the corridor and pretended to be surprised at finding them all there.

"Hey, don't you guys have homes? What're you doing still hanging around here."

"Beats me, man," Wolanski rumbled. "I was just waiting for the bus."

"Me, too," another chimed in. "It does stop here, doesn't it?"

"How about you, Mac? Why don't you take your little lady out somewhere nice and make it up to her for having to wait around."

Not thrilled at having attention suddenly directed to herself, Karla flushed. She was not feeling much like Mac's lady just then. His macho swagger might have fooled her for just a second, but no longer. She could see the taut lines on either side of his mouth and the paleness beneath his burnished tan. He was hurting, badly, but he didn't want anyone to know it.

"You're sure you're okay, Mac?" the coach asked. "I'm surprised you bounced back so fast."

"You need more faith, Willy. Since when have I let a couple of bruises ground me?"

"It's a little more than that, Mac," the coach grumbled, "as you know. But if you say you're okay —"

"I do." Firmly, he added, "I'm playing tomorrow, Willy. Count on it."

"Way to go!" one of the players exclaimed.

Wolanski nodded, a beatific smile wreathing his harsh features. "All right!"

Not until then had Karla realized the full depth of

142

the men's concern. Certainly they were worried about Mac, but they were also apprehensive about their own ability to carry on without him.

Even Bill Easton, the second-string quarterback who might have been realistically expected to relish the chance to strut his stuff in a crucial game looked relieved. He held out his hand, clasping Mac's warmly. "I'm glad you're okay, fellow. You had us worried there for a minute."

"No sweat." Good-naturedly, he added, "You'll have to wait a little longer to call the plays."

"That's fine with me," Easton told him sincerely. "Just take care of yourself."

"I plan to." Sherry-hued eyes shifted to Karla, catching her unaware. Before she could look away, he moved forward to take her arm in a light but firm grip. "Of course, I'm counting on having a little help. How about it, honey? Can I convince you to take me away from all this?"

Something flickered far in the back of his eyes, some silent plea to her to play along with the scene, not to reveal what she alone was certain he was feeling.

"Oh, I suppose," she murmured languidly. "Since I don't have anything better to do." Casting him a deliberately provocative look she knew the other players wouldn't miss, she added, "Provided, of course, that you make it worth my while."

"You heard her, men." Mac laughed. "Duty calls." The sound of relieved laughter followed them down the coridor and through the swinging doors to the parking lot.

Once outside, Mac wasted no time dropping his

swaggering pose. Eyeing her carefully, he said, "Thanks."

"For what?" she snapped, angry and not minding if he knew it. "You're a grown man. If you want to carry on like an idiot, who am I to stop you?"

"I'm not doing anything of the kind," he grumbled as they walked toward his car. Karla slowed her pace so that he could keep up without effort, but even so, she saw that his knee did not move naturally. It was stiff and unyielding, as though locked in place.

"It's the tendons again, isn't it?" she asked tightly as he unlocked the car door.

Tossing her the keys, Mac nodded. "You drive." Walking around to the passenger side, he slid in slowly, grimacing against the pain. "We'll go to your place, okay? I need to lie down for a while."

"You need your head examined," Karla muttered, turning the key in the ignition. "You don't seriously expect to play tomorrow?"

"Oh, yes, I do. You saw the looks on the guys' faces. They still don't have enough faith in themselves. If I flake out now, we could lose everything."

"What makes you think you have a choice?"

"Because I've played in worse shape than this before."

"With the team's knowledge?"

"No," he admitted grudgingly. "Brad's a stickler for that. But I can weigh the risks for myself and make up my own mind when it's worth it and when it isn't. There's no doubt it's worth it now."

Karla looked at him dubiously, all her doubts showing clearly. At his mutinous expression she stifled a sigh and said quietly, "I'm not going to try to talk you out of this. I know it would be senseless.

But at least come home with me and let me take care of you."

The look he flashed her carried equal parts of surprise and gratitude. Ruefully, he grinned. "I expected more of a struggle than that."

"Sorry to disappoint you," she muttered, "but I think you'd do better to save your strength."

"You're right." Reaching out a hand, he touched her cheek tenderly. "I just want you to know I really appreciate this. Most women would be screaming at me, and that's the last thing I need right now."

"In case you haven't noticed, I'm not most women."

Her tartness surprised him. "I didn't mean to suggest you were. Look, I'm a little out of it right now. If I say something that doesn't make any sense, I hope you'll ignore it."

"Did you . . . take anything?"

He grimaced and shook his head. "I'm not looking for any more trouble than I've already got."

"All right, then. We'll go home. I'll fix you a hot toddy, and you'll get into bed."

The grimace gave way to a reassuring leer. "Will you get in with me?"

"I'm not sure that's a good idea."

"I won't sleep right without you."

"Well, maybe . . . but only if you promise to be sensible."

He sighed woefully. "Honey, right now I don't have any choice."

Maybe not, but that didn't prevent her own instinctive response to him once they were snuggled up together in bed listening to the splatter of rain against the windows. Mac fell asleep quickly, exhausted by

145

the pain and a hefty shot of brandy. Karla lay awake, staring up at the ceiling and fighting with her conscience.

She knew, better than most, the terrible drive to go on regardless of physical considerations. At such times, the rebellious body became an enemy to be ruthlessly subdued to the will of the mind. She had done it herself, without regrets. Yet she could hardly bear to stand by and see Mac go through the same torment.

But what choice did she have? He was a grown man with the right to make his own decisions, even when they were wrong. Her love for him did not change that. She could do everything possible to help him, but nothing to control him.

Sorrow filled her as she recognized that there was only one thing in the world Mac really trusted—the pure contest of strength and will and fate on the playing field. He would risk himself there without restraint, but in every other arena—most particularly that of the heart—he kept his guard up at all times.

Until that changed, if it ever did, he would be unable to return her love. Their relationship would be restricted to the periphery of his life, never touching the essential core of his thoughts and feelings.

For a woman who lived with the very essence of emotion, transforming it through the medium of her body and spirit, that would be a slow death. Only his willingness to come to her and to reveal the pain he'd denied to everyone else gave her hope.

Gently stroking his brow, she gazed down at the proud head nestled against her breasts. He would learn now that he really could trust her; she would not betray his vulnerability even for the sake of her own peace of mind. If fate was kind, that would be the final step he had to take before being able to fully return her love.

She fell asleep, still thinking about that, and smiling.

CHAPTER NINE

Her resolve to respect Mac's right to make his own decisions wavered the next morning as he crept painfully out of bed and set about the process of trying to get himself ready to face the day.

Stiff-lipped, she ran a hot bath for him, then helped him into it. "You're crazy," she muttered, eyeing his swollen, black-and-blue knee. "Only a certified nut case would even think of walking on that, let alone trying to play."

"It looks a lot worse than it feels," he insisted, wincing as he laid back in the tub.

"Oh, sure. And pigs can fly." Kneeling down beside him, Karla touched his arm beseechingly. "Please, Mac, be sensible. You must know how much damage you can do to yourself by playing in this condition. Do you want to end up on crutches, maybe permanently?"

"That's a nice thought. Thanks for being so supportive."

His sarcasm stung. Angrily she snapped, "I am supportive, but that doesn't mean I have to ignore the risks you're taking. You're not dealing with some little groupie. I know what's at stake; a few hours of glory you could end up paying for for the rest of your life."

Scowling, Mac nudged the hot water tap with a toe as he said, "At least you remember whose life it is. I never did take well to nagging, Karla, and I'm not about to start now."

Nagging? Was that how he saw her perfectly legitimate concern? He made her sound like a shrew.

Stung, she backed away. "Fine, if that's the way you want it, I won't say another word." She had hoped to sound unconcerned, but the hurt was clear in her voice.

Mac's taut features softened slightly. He held out a hand. "Karla, I'm sorry . . ."

She would be better off to stay mad at him, but she couldn't manage it. Though she ignored the gesture and turned to leave, she said softly, "I'll start breakfast. If you need anything, holler."

Five minutes later he did just that, but only because he had no choice. *"Karla!"*

The resentful bellow warned her of what she would find as she hurried into the bathroom. He was trying, unsuccessfully, to get out of the tub. His corded arms were certainly strong enough to lift him but, unable to put any weight on his left leg, he lacked sufficient leverage.

Going quickly to his side, she tucked her shoulder under his arm and braced her slender body to take his weight. When he hesitated, she said, "Go ahead. I'm stronger than you think."

That was true but, even so, it was a strain to keep him steady until he was able to balance on one foot, his features tight with pain and inner anger, his big body shaking with frustration.

Through clenched teeth, he muttered, "What time is it?"

She didn't have to ask why he wanted to know. "You've got four hours to kickoff."

He cursed softly under his breath and began to wipe away the moisture clinging to his massive shoulders. She hesitated only a moment before taking over the task. "Let me. You sit down."

Reluctantly, he obeyed. As he stretched his injured leg out in front of him, their eyes met. His were full of pain, but nonetheless defiant. Hers pleaded silently and, she knew, uselessly.

Karla swallowed tightly. There was so much she might have said but would not. He knew how she felt; any further effort to tell him would only add to the burdens he already carried.

Her hands moved slowly over his water-cooled skin, lingering on the bunched muscles of his shoulders and the powerful sweep of his chest. The magnificently virile beauty of his form was in sharp contrast to his suffering. He was a wounded warrior, still stalwart and proud in his strength, yet mortal in his need for comfort.

She gave it willingly. Whatever she might think of his stubbornness she would not allow it to interfere with her more tender feelings. When he was dry she said quietly, "Let me shave you. That way you won't have to stand."

His rueful grin was a mark of acceptance. "Can I trust you with a razor?"

"You'll find out, won't you?" She had never shaved a man before, and found the process unexpectedly complicated. The quiet scrutiny of his knowing eyes and the patient tolerance of her novice efforts unnerved her.

All her concentration was needed to keep her hand from shaking. When she drew the razor through the last ribbon of shaving soap on his lean cheek, she breathed a sigh of relief. "There, that's better."

He ran a hand experimentally over his jaw. "Not bad. Maybe we should make this a morning ritual."

The implied reminder that their relationship was not casual warmed her. Teasingly she said, "You're spoiled enough as it is. I don't want to add to it."

His hand closed around her wrist, his callused thumb pressing lightly against the flow of her life's blood. Quietly he told her, "You already have. Being with you spoils me for all other women."

Karla looked away from him as she blushed. She wanted him so badly. The closeness of his naked body, the clean male scent of his skin, the deep timbre of his voice—all filled her with a terrible hunger.

She wanted to lie with him in the big bed and make love to him slowly and tenderly, drawing the pain from him and replacing it with ecstasy. She wanted to feel him tremble in her arms and hear the hoarse cry of her name on his lips. She wanted him to fall asleep with his head on her breasts and awaken healed.

But the world intruded, bringing harsh realities. Wiggling free of his grip, only because he permitted her to do so, she murmured, "I'll . . . fix breakfast."

Mac nodded reluctantly. Under the circumstances, his indomitable virility was both embarrassing and frustrating. Not even the considerable pain he was experiencing or all the worries that accompanied it could prevent the desire from rising in his body. The urge to stay there in the quiet, sun-filled apartment and spend the day making love with her was all but irresistible.

But he could not. Too many people were depending on him. His deeply imbued sense of honor and responsibility demanded that he meet this latest challenge with all the courage he could muster.

His determination was considerable but still just barely equal to the task. Seated side by side on the bed with Karla, the floor pillows being out of his reach, he drank coffee and tried hard not to look at her.

He didn't succeed. Time and again his gaze drifted back to the silken fall of her night-dark hair, the ivory smoothness of her skin, the slender column of her long throat, and the misleading fragility of her slender shoulders.

For all her apparent delicacy, she possessed a deeply rooted feminine strength he could not help but admire. It showed in the graceful carriage of her body and the deliberate composure of her features.

He knew she thought what he was doing was wrong, and that made him doubly grateful for her forbearance. She had come to mean so much to him that he was scared of it. How she responded to his injury was somewhat of a test, even though he knew that was unfair. If she had attempted to browbeat him into doing what she thought was right, he could have seized on that excuse to justify his reluctance to fully trust anyone, even the woman who held his heart in her small, capable hands.

He glanced at the clock beside the bed and reluctantly rose. "I'd better be going."

She nodded, pretending not to notice how the lines around his eyes and mouth tightened the instant he put any weight on his leg. "All right. I'll come along, if you don't mind."

"No, actually I'd appreciate it. You can do the driving." They were being very polite to each other. In the car, they said little. Mac asked how the ballet she was choreographing was going, and she told him everything was fine. There were problems filling some of the minor roles, and a few lingering questions in her mind about the exact sequence of movements in certain scenes, but nothing she couldn't cope with.

What she didn't tell him was that she was beginning to perceive a slow, as yet almost indistinct, deterioration of her own dancing—something she wasn't sure she could cope with. It had been coming on for a long time, and she knew it was inevitable. She was lucky to have another career already established. But not even that eased the pain of loss. She could sympathize with Mac to a degree he was not yet ready to accept.

"I hear the Tigers are tough," she said as they neared the stadium.

He shrugged dismissively. "Just one more team we have to get past to make it to the playoffs."

She knew he was understating the case. The Tigers were in fact the last team standing between the Flyers and their league playoffs. If they won that afternoon, they would have a clear shot at the Super Bowl. If they lost, it would all be over for the season.

For the younger players, that would be disappointing but not disastrous. They would have other chances in other years. But Mac wouldn't. Although he had yet to say as much, she sensed this was his final season.

She kept silent as they parked and he slid from the car. When Mac straightened up, the transformation in him was nothing short of remarkable. Strength and will shone in his eyes and in the taut power of his body. He moved easily and looked for all the world like a man with nothing more on his mind than winning a game.

Only the most observant could see the slight favoring of his left leg and the faint tenseness of his mouth. Karla wasn't fooled for a moment, but she guessed the others would be.

Resignedly she said, "I'll be waiting for you afterward. Be careful."

He nodded confidently and touched his lips to hers. "Sure thing, honey. It's going to be a great game."

"Hey, Mac," one of the other arriving players shouted, "none of that lovey-dovey stuff before kickoff. You're supposed to be lean and mean!"

"Hiya, Karla. Gonna stay for the game?"

"Wouldn't miss it."

"Great. Hey, my wife's up there in Mr. Marris's box. She's been wanting to meet you."

"Mine, too. They're gonna ask how you sweettalked us into doing that ballet stuff. Don't you tell now or there'll be no livin' with them."

Karla couldn't help but laugh. She had already met several of the players' wives and was surprised to discover that she had more in common with them than she would have expected, for they all shared the same concerns about the safety and well-being of their men. Contrary to what their husbands obviously thought, none of them needed any pointers on the care and management of football players. Everyone was an expert who could teach Karla a thing or two.

Wisely, she resisted pointing that out. With a final smile for Mac, she took herself off to the owner's box and what she hoped would be enough diversion to keep her from worrying about him in too obvious a way.

Several of the wives were already there. They greeted her warmly, introducing her to those she hadn't previously met. A white-jacketed steward arrived with refreshments. Several small children raced around, their happy shouts adding to the relaxed, optimistic mood.

"They've got a real chance today, don't they?" a chic blonde with a gentle smile said. "I'm actually starting to believe we may all be headed for Houston."

"I'm almost too nervous to even think that," another laughed. "Pete's dreamed of going to the Super Bowl ever since he was Tad's age." She grinned down at the toddler roaming around on the plushly carpeted floor near her feet. "Now he says we're really going to make it. Thanks to Mac."

"You must be so proud of him, Karla."

Uncertain how to react to that, she smiled. "Well, he is working very hard. But then they all are."

The women laughed, sympathizing with her discomfort. She could hardly accept the compliment as a wife would, yet neither could she ignore it. Their relationship was well known within the small Flyers family, as was the fact that everyone clearly approved of it.

The conversation moved on to other topics: houses, kids, the occupations of women whose men were on the road a good part of the time. Karla listened quietly, hearing the note of strength in the voices of the women.

They were all young, attractive, elegantly dressed. Many had been college cheerleaders and homecoming queens. But their storybook prettiness was deceptive. They defied stereotyping. Some were full-time homemakers, others juggled families and careers. They came from every part of the country and had traveled through all of it. Sophisticated in the best possible sense of the word, they were a congenial, intelligent group among whom Karla felt surprisingly at home.

Which was just as well, since she needed something to ease her anxiety as the minutes ticked by and game time approached. The stadium was filling up quickly. Fans who a few weeks before had been staying away were now turning out in droves to cheer the team.

Every seat was sold, meaning that the network broadcast of the game did not have to be blacked out locally. It was an amazing comeback for a team that had seemed headed for a losing season.

The Flyers came onto the field to tumultuous applause, which died down only long enough for the national anthem to be played. As the teams took up their positions on the field, Karla strained for a sight of Mac. When she did at last spot him, she stiffened in surprise.

Instead of being on the fifty-yard line for the coin

toss that decided who got the ball first, he was on the sidelines with his helmet in his hand and an angry scowl darkening his face.

Even as she watched, he approached one of the coaches and began arguing, apparently resuming a discussion begun in the locker room. The man shook his head firmly, said a few words, then motioned to the bench. Mac glowered at him and stood his ground until the coach shrugged and walked away.

Out on the field, Bill Easton was preparing for the toss. His face appeared on the TV monitor near Karla. He looked tense but determined. The excited voice of the commentator reached her as though from a great distance.

"It's official; Mac Gregor is out of the game. Rookie quarterback Bill Easton will substitute. No explanation is being given for this sudden turnaround in the team's fortunes that may well cost them a vital win."

Barely was the announcement finished than the rumble of boos could be heard through the stadium. The fans were up in arms. They had forgotten their earlier attacks on Mac and now viewed him as the hero who could take the Flyers all the way to victory in the Super Bowl. But not if he was sidelined in favor of a rookie.

"This might be some new kind of strategy," one of the wives ventured doubtfully. "To psych out the opposition by throwing them a curve?"

"It's awfully risky. All the plays key off Mac. He's the backbone of the team."

"Looks like it could be a real long day."

"Karla, do you know why they might be doing this? He is okay, isn't he?"

She didn't want to lie, but neither was she about to violate Mac's confidence. Not while there was even a dim chance that the substitution was for some reason that had nothing to do with his wayward knee. "Uh, maybe the coaches just don't want to overplay him."

The wives glanced at each other skeptically. "I suppose . . ." "Could be . . ." "But it's not like it's the start of the season. This game's important!"

"They're all important," Brad said quietly as he strolled into the box and greeted his guests. "This one just a little more so than the others. But none of them count for more than a man's health." Glancing at Karla, he said, "Mac's got a little problem with his knee. Doesn't look like anything long-term, but we want to make sure it stays that way. So he's sitting this one out."

The women nodded, not at all surprised. Brad's care of his players was a key ingredient in his popularity among their wives. They knew he would never allow—much less ask—them to play when injured. It was a standing joke among football insiders that the Flyers had the smallest drug supply cabinet of any team, a single bottle of aspirin that was expected to last all season. Their owner made sure it stayed that way.

When the curiosity had died down and attention was once more on the game, Brad leaned over to Karla and said softly, "Did he really expect to get away with it?"

"I don't know," she murmured. "But he was determined to try."

"Crazy. He could have ended up crippled."

A shiver ran through her. She had feared as much,

but that was not the same as hearing it confirmed. "And now . . . will he be all right?"

Brad laughed shortly. "He doesn't have much choice." All the while he was talking, he kept a close eye on the field. What he saw pleased him, but what was happening on the sidelines did not. Picking up the phone, he was instantly connected with the head coach. "Tell Gregor to stop jumping up. He's supposed to be sitting this one out. If he can't do it, send him to the showers."

Karla held her breath as the coach nodded and went over to Mac. They spoke briefly. Mac turned and glared up at the owner's box. He muttered something that even at that distance did not look complimentary. Limping over to the bench, he sat down.

Brad grinned and gestured for the steward to bring him a beer. "Full of vinegar, that boy. Always did like a fighter."

"It's *not* being able to fight that he doesn't like."

"I know that, but it's for his own good. Hell, how would I live with myself if I let him play and he ended up permanently disabled? He doesn't want to believe that's possible, but it is, and one of us has to realize it." He took a long swallow and watched a perfectly executed pass that put the Flyers within thirty yards of the opposition's goal.

In the brief pause between plays, Karla asked softly, "How did you find out?"

Brad shot her an indulgent look. "Granted Mac should get an Oscar for the act he put on, but I know him just a little too well to fall for it. Still, there was always a chance he might have gotten away with it. How come you didn't blow the whistle?"

The question, coming at her without any warning,

washed the color from her cheeks. Her eyes flicked from him to the man sitting so unwillingly on the sidelines and back again. "I wanted to. All last night and this morning I kept thinking I should call you. But I just couldn't do it. Mac's a grown man. I have to respect his judgment."

"Even when it stinks?"

"Yes, even then. He has a right to make his own mistakes."

"Doesn't he realize that his decisions affect more than just himself now?"

Sadly, she shook her head. "No, I don't believe he does. Or at least he's still fighting it."

Brad put a hand over hers and squeezed gently. "Sorry, honey. I should have figured it was something like that. Mac's pretty thickheaded, but he'll come around."

Karla smiled weakly. She wished she shared his confidence. While Brad was watching the game she was watching Mac, and what she saw worried her deeply.

After his black scowl in their direction, he had deliberately turned his back on the owner's box and avoided even a glance at them. Her stomach tightened as she wondered who exactly he was angry at; the man who had given the order taking him out of the game or the woman he might believe responsible?

There was little comfort in the fact that Bill Easton was doing better than anyone had a right to expect. Thrown into the breach with no warning, he was proving to be a superb quarterback.

Sensibly relying on the plays Mac had made famous and which the team could practically run with their eyes closed, he managed to put two touchdowns on the scoreboard before the end of the first half. The Flyers were leading 14–0 when they tromped down the ramp to the locker room accompanied by the heartfelt cheers of their fans.

Brad rose and held out a hand to Karla. "Come on, honey. I want to have a word with the guys, and I think you should come, too."

She hesitated only an instant. More than anything, she wanted to see Mac and to reassure herself that he didn't blame her for being sidelined. Still, she said, "I wouldn't feel comfortable going into the locker room, Brad. I know women sports reporters do it all the time, but I—"

"That's okay," he promised her as they left the box. "The coach's office is next door. You can wait there."

It was a pleasant enough room, comfortably furnished with a large oak desk, bookcases, trophy cases, and overstuffed chairs. But Karla was oblivious to her surroundings. She paced back and forth anxiously, listening to the deep male voices on the other side of the wall.

The team was obviously buoyant, riding high on Easton's unexpectedly good performance. There was much laughing and good-natured teasing, then the slow, measured tones of the coach reminding them the game wasn't won yet, and finally Brad's quiet encouragement as he expressed his faith in them.

Karla glanced up at the wall clock. Ten minutes had passed since the whistle blew ending the first half. Not many more remained before the team would be expected back on the field. If Mac was going to come to her, it had to be soon.

Even as she wondered if he would make it, the

door swung open and he limped in. His face was blank, his eyes carefully expressionless. Stiffly, he said, "Brad told me to stop by and see you."

She doubted very much that the older man would have phrased it like that, but it didn't seem worth the argument. There were more important matters to cover, like why he was looking at her as though she was a stranger he didn't particularly want to meet.

Taking a step toward him, she said softly, "Mac, I'm sorry about your being out of the game, but you must know it's for the best."

"You think so?"

"Yes. You could have ended up permanently injured."

"That was a risk I was willing to run."

"But Brad wasn't. And for that I'm grateful." She was beginning to lose patience with him, stung by his stubborn refusal to admit his own vulnerability. "If you can't see the danger—"

"Oh, I can see it all right. I just didn't want to admit it."

Karla frowned. Somehow she got the feeling he was no longer talking about the game. "What do you mean?"

"I mean," he muttered harshly, "that I let you see I was hurting when I shouldn't have. I trusted you. Hell, I was well on the way to falling in love with you!" His eyes roamed over her scornfully, making it clear that he felt he had been subject to temporary insanity and was glad to be free of it. "But you couldn't resist running to good old Brad, could you? Just out of curiosity, when did you call him? Last night or this morning?"

Before she could even attempt to answer, he raised

a hand, cutting her off. "It doesn't matter. I just wish you'd told me. Saved me the effort of coming out here. We could have stayed in bed doing what you're so very good at."

"Why you . . ." The piercing thrust of his accusations drove her into a healthy rage. How dare he speak to her like that? How dare he believe such things about her? Without thought, her hand lashed out toward his cheek.

"Careful," he warned coldly as his fingers closed around her wrist in a cruel mockery of the gentle lover's touch she had known that morning. "I'm in no mood to deal with a selfish little bitch's temper tantrum. Besides," he added mockingly, unmoved by the sudden sheen of tears in her wide blue eyes, "I'm due back on the field to lend my moral support to Easton and the rest of them."

"Then go ahead," Karla hissed. "I can do without the honor of your presence. You think I'm selfish? You win that title hands down. You can't think of anything except yourself." Scornfully she jeered, "Mac Gregor, the great quarterback. The team can't get along without him. Well, it looks like they can too, buddy. And so can I. So just get out of here."

His grip in her wrist tightened, but that pain was as nothing compared to what he was inflicting on her heart and spirit. "You know what your trouble is, Karla? You've spent too many years in your elite little world where everything happens on cue and everybody goes through their paces like tin soldiers. You're used to a bunch of regular Prince Charmings in tights who never take a step out of line. Well, I'm no Prince Charming, lady. I'm a man who isn't about to let any woman run his life."

Dropping her wrist, he grabbed his helmet and headed toward the door. "I'll have my stuff picked up from your place tomorrow." Then he was gone, up the ramp toward the stadium where the dull roar of the crowd could already be heard.

It echoed hollowly inside Karla, spiraling further and further down into an endless well of grief not all her tears would fill.

CHAPTER TEN

The human capacity for endurance in the face of overwhelming anguish continued to amaze Karla through the next few weeks. She went about her daily routine as though nothing had happened. A little quieter, perhaps, a little more introspective, but that was to be expected in light of the demands of her work.

If any of her colleagues wondered at her silence or at the occasional look of grief that passed like a shade over her features, they did not comment. She was an artist in the throes of creation and deserved privacy.

But it was not her work that drove Karla. It was the slow dying of all her hopes, the gradual yielding of the dream that Mac would relent and call her, that he would see the terrible error he had made and reach out to her.

He did not. The days passed, one after the other in gray sameness that had nothing whatsoever to do with the season. Christmas decorations appeared in the shop windows. The clear, serene voices of Salvation Army carolers rang out in the frosty air. A dusting of snow softened the harsh contours of pavement and asphalt. The scent of roasting chestnuts drifted from the carts of street vendors, swirling skyward with the steam of exhaust and the snorted breath of carriage horses lined up near Central Park.

Karla spent Christmas with friends from the ballet doing the same things she had in recent years. They exchanged gifts, went to parties, roamed around the city enjoying the sights.

She had turned down Brad's invitation to spend the holiday with him. He meant well, but she wasn't up to his sympathy, much less his barely concealed anger at Mac. He had tried to convince her to continue working with the players, apparently convinced that if she and Mac would only face each other, all their problems would be resolved.

But Karla knew better. She had gone as far as she could. To risk another confrontation with Mac in her delicate emotional state would be to court disaster.

Not wanting to let Brad know exactly how badly hurt she was, she fell back on the excuse that she had originally signed on for only six weeks and had spent longer than that with the team, so he really could not expect her to do more. He agreed grudgingly, but did not give up his efforts to bring her back into the fold.

"You have to face him some time," he insisted, "if only for your own sake. It's not like you to run away."

"I'm not running. On the contrary, I'm accepting the reality of the situation quite nicely."

Brad muttered under his breath. They were sitting

in the Russian Tea Room over a dinner he had dragged her to because he said she wasn't eating enough. He was right.

It was two days after Christmas, and she was wearing the crimson sweater dress a girl friend had given her. A few weeks before it would have fit perfectly, emphasizing the slender purity of her curves. But instead it hung rather loosely, giving her a fragile air that made Brad scowl.

"I'd like to string Gregor up," he rasped. "And I would, too, if I didn't know how miserable he is."

This was not the first allusion Brad had made to Mac's alleged unhappiness. Karla let it pass, just as she had all the others. She simply didn't believe them. Mac was back in the game, his knee completely well, and the Flyers' winning streak continued unbroken. Just the day before, they had won the divisional semifinals. Only one more match remained between them and the Super Bowl.

"I'll bet you're looking forward to Houston," she said in a deliberate bid to change the subject.

Brad scowled. He took a bite of his crepes with red caviar and sour cream and said, "That's a way off yet. We may not make it."

"I think you will," Karla assured him quietly. She did not really want the vodka he had ordered for her because he said she looked cold, but the sip she took eased the dryness in her throat. Softly she admitted, "I saw the last game. The team is fantastic."

He grunted almost inaudibly but looked pleased. "I was wondering how you could stay away completely after all you put in to helping us win."

"I didn't have much to do with it," she demurred.

"Nonsense. If you hadn't come along when you did, they'd still be tripping over their own feet."

Despite herself, Karla laughed. "You know they weren't that bad to start with. They just needed a little time."

"That's what Mac said." The chagrined look she shot him made him laugh. "My dear wife, God rest her soul, always said that when I got fixed on something I was worse than a dog with a bone. I'm convinced you and Mac belong together, and your refusal to admit it doesn't change a thing."

"Please . . . I don't want to talk about this."

"I know you don't. But sooner or later we've got to." He was silent for a moment before he murmured, "I was responsible for the two of you meeting. How do you think I feel now, knowing how badly he's hurt you?"

Karla looked up from her plate where her smoked salmon remained all but untouched. She didn't quite believe he was as remorseful as he sounded, but she felt compelled to give him the benefit of the doubt.

"What happened between Mac and me has nothing to do with you. It was just one of those unfortunate things that crop up every once in a while. We're simply too different to get along, and we should have realized it from the beginning."

Brad raised an eyebrow skeptically. "Different? The two of you have more in common than just about anyone I know."

"That's ridiculous. We come from completely different worlds."

"Do you? You've both made your way in very demanding professions through a combination of sheer physical talent and grueling work. You're dedi-

168

cated, ambitious, and highly disciplined. Both of you are also realistic enough to see what lies ahead and to plan for it accordingly. That's why you've gotten into choreography and Mac is signing on as a coach."

"Is that what he's doing?"

"Yes, but I won't bore you with the details. After all, you don't want to talk about him."

"Sometimes you are the most annoying man."

He grinned unrepentantly. "It's part of my boyish charm."

"*Ha!* It's part of your absolute determination to get your own way."

"Well . . . maybe a little. Stop me if I'm boring you, but the fact is, Mac knows this is his last season. He realized that even before the first game. Some men would try to hang on past their prime, but he's too smart for that. He'll move on to the next logical step in his career, coaching for the Flyers."

"And you're both happy with that?"

"I sure am. I've got more respect for Mac than just about any man I know. He'll be a real asset. But as to how happy he's feeling—"

"He must be. I had an idea all along coaching was what he wanted."

"Hmmm. He seemed pleased enough, until the last few weeks. Lately, he just goes around scowling and so tightly wound up everybody's afraid to say boo to him."

"Why would he do that when you're winning?"

"You know perfectly well why. The man misses you in the worst way possible, but he's too pigheaded to admit it. Now, are you going to be as cussed stubborn as him or are you grown up enough to do what's right for you both?"

"And just what do you think that is?"

"Go see him," Brad said promptly. "Talk out whatever's caused the trouble between you."

Karla was shaking her head even as he spoke. "I can't. You don't understand. There's just too much distrust between us."

"Are you saying you don't trust Mac?"

"No . . . I had complete faith in him. Maybe that was my mistake. I really thought that all he needed was time and patience to get over his reluctance about really opening himself up to another person. He accused me once of getting upset at him because he had punctured my neat little world. And he was right. But he has the same problem. For years he's been completely self-contained. He doesn't know how to stop . . . doesn't even want to."

"I think you're wrong about that," Brad said gently. "If I read the situation right, and I'm sure I do, he wants to share everything with you. He just doesn't know how to go about it."

"If that's true, then why did he grab the first excuse he could to break off with me?" At Brad's surprised look she said, "You must have figured out by now that he thinks I told you about his knee. He held me responsible for getting him sidelined and he wasted no time telling me what he thought of that." She shivered slightly. "I never even got a chance to defend myself, not that I would have. If he can't have faith in me, then nothing else we've shared matters."

"I didn't realize what he thought," Brad said slowly. "He never mentioned it to me. I just presumed there was some problem." He shook his head angrily. "That young idiot. Doesn't he have enough sense to realize you'd never do such a thing?"

"Apparently not," she said sadly.

"I should have guessed . . . should have said something to him."

"No, you have no part in this. It's strictly between Mac and me. If it hadn't been that business with his knee, it would have been something else. As long as he couldn't trust me, we didn't have a chance."

"Karla, you have to try to understand. Mac's had a hard road. I'm not trying to make excuses for him, but he learned at an early age to depend strictly on himself. And ever since he got to the top, the women he's met . . . well, let's just say they weren't the type to inspire great trust or loyalty."

"I know that."

"So you see, if you'd just try, just give him another chance . . ."

Sadly, Karla shook her head. "No, Brad. I know you mean well, but it wouldn't work. I did everything I could. To do more would be to destroy all my self-respect. Without that, I wouldn't be any good for Mac, so there's no point."

"All right, honey. I'm not going to argue with you. There's just one thing I hope you're keeping in mind! You've based your whole life on discipline and self-control that are admirable by themselves and have enabled you to do more than most people can even dream of. In that way, you and Mac are very much alike. But there comes a time when you have to break training and go with your instincts, take a risk."

Before she could comment, he held up a hand. "I know I'm upsetting you and I don't want to do that, so let's drop it. There's something else I want to talk with you about, anyway, something very important to me that I would really like you to do."

Feeling guilty about having disappointed him, she was predisposed to agree to whatever else was on his mind. But she still wasn't prepared when he said, "If the team wins in the finals next week, come to Houston with us. All the guys miss you and your support could turn out to be crucial."

"That's ridiculous. You can't make me believe for a moment that they need me to win the Super Bowl."

"Come on now, Karla. You know what it's like to be going for the really big one, with everything you've got on the line. At times like that, even the tiniest edge can make all the difference in the world. Would you really deny them that?"

"Brad, what you're saying doesn't make any sense. The team doesn't need me. I've done everything I can for them. They've probably forgotten all about me."

"They talk about you all the time, and the wives keep asking how you are."

"Really?"

"Yep. They mention you in front of Mac, too. I think they do that on purpose 'cause they're mad at him for being such a fool."

"They blame him for our breaking up?" That didn't seem right. Surely his teammates should side with him.

"Sure do. Why, Wolanski told him just the other day that if Mac didn't get back together with you, he was even a bigger fool than everyone thought." He laughed. "Believe me, that didn't go down real well. Mac went through practice at a low boil. Practically ribbed the stuffing out of one of the tackle dummies."

She eyed him skeptically. "You wouldn't be making all this up, would you?"

Affronted, he withdrew into his dignity. "How could you even suggest such a thing? I agreed we'd forget all about this little problem you and Mac are having."

"It's not little. It's—"

"A closed subject. What we're talking about now is whether or not you'll come to Houston to support the team, for my sake and theirs."

"You," she told him frostily, "are being very unfair."

"So sue me. I'm just an old man with no family of my own, no one to share a wonderful moment with . . ."

"*Old?* Don't try to pull that lonely old codger routine on me. Every woman in this room has been giving you the eye ever since we sat down."

"Really?" He couldn't help but look pleased.

She laughed wryly. "You're absolutely incorrigible, you know that? You'll do anything to get your own way, even try to play on my nonexistent sympathy. Well, forget it. It won't work."

A look of genuine dismay clouded his eyes. "Karla, I only meant—"

"I'll go to Houston, but not because I'm silly enough to believe any of that nonsense about you and the team needing me. I'll go because I want to." The moment the words were out she was surprised, but no more so than Brad. He stared at her in rueful astonishment.

"It takes a lot of guts to be honest with yourself."

"The alternative is worse." She remembered when she had said that to Mac and sighed. "If I don't go,

173

I'll always wonder if I stayed away because I was afraid."

"You're not a coward, honey."

"Didn't somebody say 'love makes cowards of us all'?"

"It can also make us stronger and more courageous than we could ever manage on our own." Covering her hand, Brad said quietly, "You had a brief glimpse of something very special. Maybe you're right and it was just an illusion that can't be recaptured. But just maybe you're wrong. Can you afford to take that risk?"

Reluctantly, Karla shook her head. She knew she couldn't. Sitting there, listening to Brad talk about Mac, she had realized how desperately she needed to see him again, to hear his voice and to convince herself that he really was all right. She would risk the pain of seeing him. She had to.

So softly that he could barely hear her, she murmured, "I'll go to Houston, Brad. But not by myself. The Flyers will have to win the playoffs."

A tender smile lit his eyes. "Better start packing."

Five days later his prophetic words proved true as Mac led his team to a stunning divisional victory that had sportswriters in an uproar and fans lined up for blocks to buy tickets to the Super Bowl.

Karla had watched the game on TV, having once again refused Brad's invitation to join him in his box. She couldn't explain that the strain of seeing Mac, even from a distance, was too much to be endured in public. How she would manage in Houston, she didn't know. But she would find out soon.

Coming off the field, accepting the wild acclaim of the fans and his teammates, he looked tired and somehow depressed. That gave her a slim ray of hope even as she worried about him.

Perhaps his knee was hurting. Perhaps there was something wrong with his family back in West Virginia. Perhaps he was regretting his fast-approaching retirement. Perhaps he missed her . . .

She resolutely shied away from that thought. It was pointless to indulge herself in fantasies, not when the reality might turn out to be worse than anything she had yet encountered. She was not so naive that she didn't realize that Mac might not be alone in Houston.

That thought continued to haunt her as she reluctantly packed. She planned to bring as few clothes as possible, telling herself she was only going for one night and wouldn't need much. She would arrive the day of the game, stay for what would hopefully be a victory celebration, and then depart.

Even such a brief visit would not save her from seeing Mac. What would his reaction be? Would he be glad she was there, or indifferent or angry?

She really didn't think she could face his anger again, yet she might have no choice. The image of him mocking her for chasing after him made her cringe. If he did that, would he be right? Was that what she was doing?

All the way down on the plane she told herself it didn't matter. Whatever her motives for going to Houston, they centered on her responsibility for herself and her own future. She had discovered in the blank, arid weeks without Mac that she simply couldn't put him out of her mind. Nothing else took the place she hadn't even known was empty before he came.

If her work had been going badly as a result of their estrangement, she might have been able to fool herself, to pretend that once she got her career back on track, she would recover. But that wasn't the case.

A rueful smile softened her mouth as she accepted a drink from the steward and reflected on the old cliché about artists having to suffer to achieve their full potential.

Houston was everything she remembered from visits there on ballet tours: vibrant and pulsing with energy. In her present mood, it was all a bit much. By the time she checked into the hotel near the Astrodome, she felt wrung out and more than ready for a shower and a nap.

She got the first but not the second. As she was wrapping a terry-cloth robe around herself, someone knocked at the door. Opening it, she found a bellboy holding a crystal vase full of long-stemmed roses.

"Ms. Morley?"

"That's right. Come in." Standing aside for him to pass, she gestured toward the chest of drawers set against one wall of the large, elegantly appointed room. "You can put those over there."

He did so, then politely refused the tip she offered. "No thanks, ma'am. It's all taken care of."

Showing him out, Karla could not resist a grin. Trust Brad to guess how she would be feeling and find some way to cheer her up. The lush blossoms were a deep, velvety red. Their fragrance filled the room, bringing a memory of soft spring days into the sterility of the hotel room.

Breathing in their scent appreciatively, she looked for a card and was surprised to discover there was none. Perhaps he had forgotten or thought it wasn't necessary.

Shrugging, she switched on the TV while contemplating whether or not she should call room service for a snack. Before she could decide, her appetite evaporated as Mac's face suddenly swam into focus before her. She sat down hard on the edge of the bed and watched what turned out to be an interview taped the previous day.

Yes, he thought the Flyers had an excellent chance of winning the Super Bowl. Yes, he expected to be in the starting lineup for the game. He was in good shape and saw no reason why he should not play well.

Karla wasn't convinced of that. He looked even more tired and tightly strung than he had a few days before. There were new lines around his mouth and eyes, and he seemed to have lost weight, hardly wise at a time when he needed all his strength and endurance.

No, he wasn't overly concerned about the Titans' legendary defense. They deserved respect, but the Flyers could handle them. No, he didn't have anything to say about his plans for next season. He was still undecided.

She wasn't surprised by that. Mac wouldn't announce his intentions in such a setting. He would wait and do it properly, with Brad at his side. What did surprise her was his reaction when the interviewer rather coyly asked if his social life was as quiet as it looked to outsiders.

"The lovely ladies of New York say they're pining away for you, Mac. All your old haunts miss you, and there hasn't been a mention of your name in the

177

gossip columns for months. Is the rumor that you've settled on one very special lady true?"

Instead of replying with the cool insouciance she would have expected, Mac hesitated. A flicker of pain shone in his eyes as he finally said, "For once, I have to admit the rumor mill is right. There is a very special lady in my life. The only problem is, I'm not sure I'm in hers."

The interviewer wasn't prepared for such candor. He fumbled a moment before regaining his bright, empty smile. "Well, thanks a lot, Mac. We all sure wish you the best, on the field and off." Grinning, he took it upon himself to add, "If that special lady is listening, maybe she'll decide to let you in."

Maybe she already had, Karla thought glumly as she switched off the set. Maybe she already knew she had given in too soon instead of fighting for a prize that was well worth any effort to attain. Maybe that was why she was sitting in a hotel room with tears on her cheeks and a silly grin on her face.

A moment longer she sat, staring at the blank set and thinking about what Mac had said and how he had looked. Okay, he wasn't exactly Prince Charming. He should have trusted her and, failing that, should have given her a chance to explain. But he hadn't and now she had a choice: hold it against him forever or try again.

It wasn't much of a contest. Jumping up, she flipped her suitcase open and began rummaging through it, looking for the azure jump suit that fit her like a second skin and was absolutely the only thing to wear to a Super Bowl victory.

178

CHAPTER ELEVEN

Before Karla could get out of the room, the bellboy returned with another vase of flowers, also minus a card. He grinned at her as he set it down on the dresser.

"I guess someone knows you like roses, ma'am."

"Looks that way." He refused another tip and left before she could ask if he knew who was sending them. On reflection, she decided she already had a pretty good idea. Brad might send one bouquet to reward her for being brave enough to come. He wouldn't send two. Only a defunct Prince Charming would do that.

Plucking one of the blossoms from the vase, she pinned it to her jump suit, took a final look at herself in the mirror, and grinned. Her hair fell loosely over her shoulders, a softly curled tendril reaching toward the open V neck that showed just a hint of cleavage. Her eyes sparkled, their deep blue hue intensified by the color she wore. Her body looked firm and supple, curved in all the right places.

At least, the men in the elevator thought so. Rarely had she been so appreciatively scrutinized. It amused her to discover she didn't mind a bit. All her attention was on Mac, and how he would react when he saw her.

But before that could happen there was the little detail of a championship game to get through. Her arrival at the owner's box was greeted by waves and hugs from the wives who seemed not at all surprised to see her. The champagne was already flowing, and she took a sip of the glass Brad handed her as she met his amused gaze calmly.

"So I'm here. Don't tell me you're surprised."

"No," he admitted, "just glad." Quietly, he added, "And I won't be the only one."

"I haven't seen him yet," she explained as she slid into a seat. "It didn't seem like a good idea before the game."

"Good Lord, no! Let's keep him nice and mean for the Titans."

"Is that how you expect him to be?"

"Honey, I'm counting on it. Unless I miss my guess, Mac will go out on the field and let loose with all the frustration he's been storing up the last few weeks. Should be quite a show."

It was. Days later, sports commentators and armchair quarterbacks were still talking about what came to be known as "Gregor's Game." Maybe that wasn't strictly fair to the other players, but no one seemed to mind.

Not when Mac threw pass after pass straight into the arms of his waiting receivers, marching his team

180

down the field in a relentless assault that left the crowd gasping. His control was absolute, as was the brilliance of the strategy he faultlessly executed.

No one watching him could believe he was in anything but his prime. He was going out in glory, and Karla loved him all the more for it. The Titans, who were coming off a triumphant season, were stunned. Whatever they tried, whoever they sent against him, nothing worked.

The statistics told the story. By the end of the first half, the Flyers had carried the ball for twenty-four minutes versus their opponents' six. They had passed for two hundred yards, a Super Bowl record, and scored two touchdowns and a field goal to bring the score to 17–0.

Brad was fairly bouncing up and down in his seat with excitement. He raced off to the locker room to confer with the team, returning with a broad grin on his face and fresh bottles of champagne. "I swear, Mac's out to break every record in the book. I'm almost sorry for the Titans."

The second half was even better than the first, with the Flyers switching back and forth between passing and rushing games so adroitly that they were impossible to keep up with.

By the last quarter, the opposition's intense frustration was showing. On every play, the ground was littered with penalty flags as the referees struggled to enforce the rules.

Mac was hit twice after releasing the ball, clear violations that cost the Titans a total of twenty yards. Even that didn't stop them. They were desperate and it showed.

Karla was on the edge of her seat during the final

minutes. The win was assured by a score of 28–3. But she was terrified that Mac might be hurt. His teammates apparently had a similar concern. Their screening of him was even more effective than usual. Younger players hurled themselves relentlessly into opposing blockers in all-out efforts to protect him.

It worked. As the crowd shouted off the last seconds before swarming down onto the field, Mac was unhurt, on his feet, and triumphant. With the final whistle, he was hoisted onto his teammates' shoulders and carried off with the game ball in hand.

In the owner's box it was difficult to tell who was more thrilled, Brad or the wives. Champagne corks popped, everybody hugged everybody else, and the flash of brilliant smiles was almost blinding.

Even as she did her share of hugging and smiling, Karla could think of nothing except what Mac would say when he saw her again. The large color TV in the box showed the scene in the Flyers' locker room. Brad had hurried down there to share the glory of his team. He was standing next to Mac, grinning broadly, his arm around the younger man's shoulders looking for all the world like a proud father with his son.

There were the usual comments about what it felt like to win a Super Bowl, gracious assurances that the other team was still worthy of respect, and some technical stuff about strategy Karla didn't bother to try to follow.

Instead she wondered at the difference between Mac's manner and that of the rest of the men. They were all ebullient, riding high on the fulfillment of a lifelong dream. He looked more relieved than happy, and oddly wary.

She touched the rose pinned to her jump suit and smiled. The other women's eyes were all glued to the TV set. It was an easy matter to slip out unnoticed.

Leaving the owner's box, she was waylaid by a delivery boy carrying a long white box. "Ms. Morley?"

She nodded briskly. "Is there a card on that one?"

"Huh? Oh, a card. Yeah. Here."

Her fingers trembled as she opened it and read the words.

> Wanted: Retired quarterback seeks position as Prince Charming to very special lady. No experience but willing to learn.

A radiant smile spread across her features. With the flowers in her arms, Karla hurried away. If her calculations were correct, it would be at least an hour before Mac would decently shake loose from the interviewers and TV cameras and make his way back to the hotel. By then she would be ready.

In fact, only forty-five minutes had passed when the knock sounded at her door. She bit her lip as she walked toward it. The ivory silk of her ankle-length gown rustled softly around her legs as she moved. What had possessed her to bring the antique peignoir she could not imagine. Sheer feminine instinct, perhaps, or maybe indomitable hopefulness.

Cobweb-fine lace began at her throat and spread down over the arch of her shoulders clear to the crest of her high, pointed breasts. Long billowing sleeves were caught at the wrists by seed pearl buttons. The alabaster perfection of her body shone clearly through silk so delicate as to be almost transparent.

183

Her hand on the doorknob, she hesitated a moment. If she was wrong, she was going to be very embarrassed. She shrugged lightly. As Brad had said, sometimes you just had to break training and take risks.

She opened the door wide, standing framed in its archway, to the hungrily appreciative gaze of the man who stood before her. "Karla . . ."

For a man who had just played four quarters of championship football he looked remarkably fresh. A taupe silk shirt hugged the powerful span of his chest above elegantly tailored gray slacks. A few drops of water clung to his thick chestnut hair, evidence of a recent shower. Beneath his burnished tan, his high-boned cheeks were slightly flushed. The gleam in his golden eyes was infinitely male, yet tinged with uncertainty.

Clearing his throat, he said, "I understand you have a vacancy for a Prince Charming."

Karla let her gaze roam over him ardently for a long moment before she recollected herself enough to smile. Standing aside, she silently invited him to step into the room. He did so hastily, without ever taking his eyes from her.

Before closing the door and locking it securely, she slipped the DO NOT DISTURB sign into place, then turned to smile at him tenderly. It was very quiet in the room. There was only the soft woosh of silk as she closed the distance between them and was caught up in his arms, a husky groan breaking from him as he drew her to him, and the ardent words of lovers at last truly together.

"I'm sorry," he murmured, his head buried in the

fragrant softness of her hair. "I should never have said what I did."

"Doesn't matter," she murmured, her hands trailing over his corded back, savoring the latent strength of his huge body. So powerful, yet so gentle. Only one of the many contrasts that made him an endless source of fascination. She would spend a lifetime getting to know him fully and never regret a moment of it.

His mouth found hers in a long, hungry kiss that made it clear he had suffered every bit as much from their separation as she had. "I know we should talk," he rasped, "clear the air."

Her fingers were already on the buttons of his shirt, making short work of them. "Later."

Later there would be time for everything. Just then only one thing mattered. Mac grinned down at her, in complete accord.

His big hands were remarkably gentle as he slipped the peignoir from her. They shook slightly as they roamed over her naked body, bringing her instantly to an almost painful state of arousal. But his huge arms were rock-steady as he lifted her to the bed and gently laid her down.

As he quickly stripped off his clothes, she watched him unabashedly. He was so magnificently male that her breath caught in her throat. She raised her arms, beseeching him to come to her.

His intense need for her was unmistakable, but it did not prompt him to haste. Lying beside her on the bed, he propped himself up on an elbow and surveyed her intently. His ardent scrutiny made her blush, prompting a purely male chuckle.

"I thought you were used to being looked at."

She took a swat at his nose. "Not like this."

"Then we'll have to get you used to it, because you are definitely the best view in town."

Despite her prone position on the bed, she managed a teasing bow. "Thank you, kind sir. But there's something you should know about this view." He raised an eyebrow quizzically. "It's eminently touchable."

"Oh, yes," he rasped, reaching out a big hand to stroke lightly the slender line of her arm. "Like warm satin. I never knew skin could be this soft until I met you." His grin returned, though a bit shakily. "Or that it could be designed so perfectly."

"You're not put together so badly yourself," Karla murmured. His feathery caresses were sending shock waves of pleasure through her, making her yearn for more.

Giving in to the temptation to touch him, she spread her fingers over the bulging muscles of his upper chest. The thick mat of hair felt like a furry pelt. She remembered the velvet roughness of it against her breasts and trembled.

Mac moved so swiftly that she was caught by surprise. Pressing her onto her back, he lowered his body on top of hers, making her vividly aware of his size and strength. "I wanted to take this slowly," he groaned, "make it last. But I can't. You're too much for me. I've got to have you . . . now. . . ."

Callused palms cupped her breasts, the thumbs stroking her aching nipples. With the ferocity—and the finesse—he had demonstrated so brilliantly on the playing field, he claimed her mouth, parting her lips with his and piercing her with the moist thrust of his tongue.

186

He gave her no time to adjust to one exquisite sensation before initiating another. A powerful thigh eased between hers, pressing upward against her soft nest of curls. A hand slipped beneath her, squeezing her buttocks as he arched her even closer.

"Sweetheart," he groaned huskily, "tell me if you aren't ready."

But she was more than ready. Her body was crying out for him, desperately craving the surcease only he could give. Catching his face in her hands, she raised him to her.

"Come to me, Mac, please. I can't bear to be so empty. . . ."

He stared down at her, his features taut with need yet his eyes cautious, gauging her willingness. His hand moved gently, making absolutely certain her arousal was as great as his own.

An instant later the emptiness was filled as he moved within her, first slowly, then with increasing wildness matched by her own uninhibited joyful response.

In a tangle of arms and legs, caressing hands, and seeking lips they raised each other to a pinnacle of shattering joy where they poised through long, endless moments before soaring together into the furtherest reaches of complete fulfillment.

Mac was masterful and tender, demanding and giving, all male and infinitely human. Karla opened for him completely, withholding nothing, telling him with her body and her spirit how much she loved him.

They said it to each other over and over, in words and in touch. "I love you," he murmured at the moment that he entered her. "I love you," she cried as they moved perfectly together as though to ancient music only they could hear.

"I love you," he groaned in the instant the world shattered around them, and they were alone in a perfect universe of their own creation.

"I love you," she breathed as they settled slowly back to earth wrapped in each other's arms.

An eternity later, he raised himself to smile down at her flushed face and sparkling eyes. A callused finger stroked the curve of her cheek wonderingly as he nestled her within the protective curve of his body.

"Now, about that Prince Charming job . . ."

Karla laughed softly, a sound of pure joy and contentment rippling on the quiet air. Her hands stroked his damp back as she listened to the cherished sound of his heartbeat.

Somewhere in the farther reaches of the hotel a victory celebration was in progress, and back in New York fans were undoubtedly rejoicing. She was happy for them, happy for the whole world, happy most of all for herself and Mac and the magic they had found together.

Her strong, slender body arched toward him as she drew his head down to hers. Passion, great enough to last a lifetime and beyond, surged again within them. "It's all yours."

CANDLELIGHT Ecstasy Supreme

☐ 29 **DIAMONDS IN THE SKY**, Samantha Hughes..................11899-9-28

☐ 30 **EVENTIDE**, Margaret Dobson 12388-7-24

☐ 31 **CAUTION: MAN AT WORK**, Linda Randall Wisdom 11146-3-37

☐ 32 **WHILE THE FIRE RAGES**, Amii Lorin.......................19526-8-14

☐ 33 **FATEFUL EMBRACE**, Nell Kincaid 12555-3-13

☐ 34 **A DANGEROUS ATTRACTION**, Emily Elliott 11756-9-12

☐ 35 **MAN IN CONTROL**, Alice Morgan 15179-1-20

☐ 36 **PLAYING IT SAFE**, Alison Tyler..................................16944-5-30

$2.50 each